SOON
COME

SOON COME

KUBA SHAND-BAPTISTE

dialogue
books

DIALOGUE BOOKS

First published in Great Britain in 2025 by Dialogue Books
An imprint of John Murray Press

1

Hardback ISBN 978-0-349-70497-5

Typeset in Berling by M Rules
Printed and bound in Great Britain by Clays Ltd, Elcograf S.p.A.

John Murray policy is to use papers that are natural, renewable and
recyclable products and made from wood grown in sustainable forests.
The logging and manufacturing processes are expected to conform to the
environmental regulations of the country of origin.

Carmelite House   The authorised representative
50 Victoria Embankment   in the EEA is
London EC4Y 0DZ   Hachette Ireland
                                     8 Castlecourt Centre
                                  Dublin 15, D15 XTP3, Ireland
                                     (email: info@hbgi.ie)

www.dialoguebooks.co.uk

John Murray Press, part of Hodder & Stoughton Limited
An Hachette UK company

For Mummy and Daddy

Chapter One: The Funeral

(Notting Hill, 1959)

Mikey had never seen this many people on the streets of his neighbourhood. And moving so slowly. Dressed in their funeral best, the congregation outside appeared sheepish, awkward, frightened. As if lining up for a thwack round the ear, or a verbal one. 'A wah kinda foolishness?' – his mother's favourite admonition whenever he did something she didn't understand or like. He was always using any paper he could find in the flat to sketch his ships – always ships. But Mikey's mother didn't see a budding artist; she saw a little brat forever scribbling on the backs of letters and bills. She'd shout, and down his head would hang like the mourners outside.

He knew why they looked like that. Head in the clouds as his was, Mikey was a solid fourteen years old, and understood, in part, the ugliness of what surrounded their little world of family and friends. A man had died. A man had been murdered. Everyone had been discussing it for weeks, a murmur of suspicion wafting through the streets of Notting Hill and Ladbroke Grove.

Now, while the freshly pressed suits and smocks made their funeral walk, the west London rumour mill had become quiet and reflective. Whatever conjecture there had been about who did it – the Teddy Boys? Possibly. A lone racist? Maybe. Mosley's lot? Probably – had now been replaced by shoulder-shaking sobbing and disbelief.

Mikey felt his mother walk into the living room and freeze. Apparently it wasn't for an impromptu nag or instruction. She stayed silent. Of the million things Mikey found fascinating his mother feared that this murder, something she could barely make sense of herself, would pique his curiosity to an extreme that no stern look or strike with a wooden spoon would stop.

She was right. Mikey had been staring out of that window for a good twenty minutes. The light from the sun had created a halo around his wiry, almost copper afro and reduced his sinewy body to a blue silhouette. His head was cocked to the side, as if asking: 'so *this* is what happens to us here?'

'Mi nuh know weh yuh ah look pon so 'ard, pickney,' his mother said, poorly concealing her fear. He didn't answer. They'd discussed this some days before. Mikey had already gone through the feelings of disappointment and uselessness when he was told he couldn't perform his altar-boy duties at St Michael's church for Mr Cochrane's service. It was the singing he'd miss the most, the chance to show off his ever-expanding range, though he wouldn't dare admit that out loud. But he knew deep down why she was uneasy. This – like the dingy, unfriendly, cold city London had revealed itself to be on his arrival – was something she could build him up to withstand, but not protect him from. He knew it. The way she was looking at him now – eyes bulging and mouth drooping – confirmed as much. Their worst fears were laid out with Mr Cochrane's body at the funeral, latently present in the sounds of mourning from the street below.

Still Mikey was curious. He observed the flowers. So many of them: carnations, chrysanthemums, lilies; a carnival of colour compared to the black, grey and navy suits, the starched, sensible dresses. He saw people: Black, white, Indo-Caribbean, and in between. Mothers with babies, men wielding papers with the words: *TIME TO HIT BACK*, splashed across the front in big, bold capital letters as jittery onlookers, dreading the repeat of what led to Kelso's – Mr Cochrane's – death in the first place, watched. This wasn't your average farewell to the elderly or the sick: too much anger in the air. Kelso had been thirty-two. The appetite for retribution was growing. It felt like a morbid afterglow of the fighting from the year before, when the white boys and the Union Movement fascists daubed walls and doors with *KBW* (Keep Britain White) and screamed promises of lynchings into the night sky. Mikey had watched those scenes unfold from street corners just far enough away from the action to avoid getting caught up in it. He'd watched from this same window where, in the distance, he saw crowds clashing and Molotov cocktails flying.

Continuing to peer out of the rickety single-panel windowpane that felt as if it might give way each time he pressed his button nose against it, Mikey wondered what the people below were talking about. Some stood off to the side, groups of men in a line leaning against the cool stone walls of the church and speaking out the sides of their mouths as if too broken to maintain eye contact.

Two men caught his attention. A young Black boy, perhaps

sixteen, which would be two years older than he was, eyed the clergymen ahead, their elaborate vestments flapping in the wind as the boy's face grew more perplexed. An older man, possibly his father, approached the boy and said something to him. The boy shook his head. The man ruffled his springy hair. Mikey, still being watched by his mother, couldn't shake his intrigue. What could they possibly be saying on a day like this? What else was there, apart from 'I'm sorry'?

Heavy footsteps and the faint stench of Guinness roused Mikey from his daydreaming, alerting him, minutes after he thought she'd left the front room, to the return of his mother with his father, now slowly making his way through the door to their flat and up the stairs. Mikey and his father made eye contact.

'Hello, Daddy,' said Mikey, just sincerely enough to get away with turning straight back to the spectacle.

'Lard, yuh see how many people come out for this?' His father clunked down on the thin-framed settee and stretched out his short, thick legs with difficulty. He'd put on weight in the last few months, and his favourite smart suit had become a tad snug since he last fished it out.

'How many do you think there are?'

'Mi nuh know. Tink mi did ear one of the policemen saying it two thousand, maybe more.'

'How was the service?' said Mikey's mother in a tone that they all knew meant she didn't really want to know. Mikey's father shrugged, said something about it being sad and grabbed at the brown paper bag, damp with conden-sation, he'd brought in with him, took the glass bottle of Guinness inside it to his lips. He guzzled the foamy, tart dregs with pleasure. Some of it landed on the left lapel of his suit. He watched it dissolve and spread into a stain, then half-heartedly tried to brush it away with his fingertips. He was a little drunk, a rarity for him. Mikey's mother, who'd been watching and silently judging for the past couple of minutes, handed her husband a damp dish cloth and shot him a knowing look. He accepted it without breaking eye contact and flashed a forlorn smile back.

'They're leaving now,' Mikey said, rising slowly from his spot to claim space next to his father on the settee.

'Already? The body in the hearse and everything?' Mikey shrugged. His father stumbled to his feet to get a glimpse from the window. 'Yeah, they're moving,' Mikey's father offered, searching his teeth for pieces of lodged food from breakfast.

'They're heading to Kensal Green cemetery. Shine and dem seh dem ah come link me soon, but mi nuh really feel like going too tough.'

'You're not going to the graveside?' Mikey's mother chimed in, trying her best to hide her disappointment while she fluffed the limp, indigo, circular cushions on the doily-covered settee.

Mikey knew where this was going. His mother's brow furrowing deeper with every second. She'd be going on about the need to represent the family next, the importance of being respectful at a time like this. Bullshit – he'd be down there himself if she'd let him.

'Mi nuh know ... it would be nice to have someone go fi the family.'

'Send the pickney then,' said Mikey's father, without skipping a beat.

Mikey guffawed. His mother kissed her teeth and slipped away into the bedroom, her anger driven home by the violent squeak the bed spring let out when she forcefully slammed her backside onto the mattress. Taking it as his cue to make things better, Mikey's father dragged himself off the settee and trudged in after her.

Half an hour later, save for the scratch of Mikey's pencil against the smooth, glossy piece of paper he'd salvaged from the scrap drawer, the flat had fallen silent. The crowd outside had mostly gone, though people still lingered in the streets, a faint chatter in the air. Mikey had lost interest in watching. He was still on the sofa, trying to remember the exact curves of the ship he'd arrived here on. A monster of a thing that raised his heart rate, his hopes, his dreams all at the same time. He could still hear the waves lapping against the ship's bow as it cut through the Caribbean Sea. He could smell the stink of seawater around him. The feel of the ocean's spray on his skin, creating a light film of chalky, salty dust once it dried. He could also hear what sounded like crying. Not from the deep recesses of his imagination, but from his parents' bedroom.

The noise cut through him like a bone saw. He knew immediately, despite never hearing it before, who it was coming from. Gut-wrenching, the wailing was loud and deep, even if it was muffled. It was his father. He was sure of it. His mother's sobs had never had so much bass. Enough reminiscing. He was going to investigate.

This was the sort of thing that got Mikey in trouble. 'That nose of yours,' his mother would say to him, 'is always sniffing around someone else's business.' An expert at eavesdropping on to these conversations without detection, he slithered onto the floor and crawled along the spotless floorboards towards his parents' room, where the sobbing had been replaced by sniffling.

The bed creaked. Mikey froze, readying his limbs for a sudden dash should one of them choose to cut their conversation short. False alarm. The chatting continued. Through the crack of their bedroom door, left ajar as it always was in this household ('wah yuh ah talk bout *privacy*, Mikey? The only door yuh need fi shut is the one fi the washroom' – another gem from his mother) he spotted his parents in an embrace he'd never seen the like of. The blinds and the light from the big window had created golden brown and black stripes all over their bodies. His mother was cradling his father's head, and he was letting her. She rocked back and forth on the edge of the small double, whispering words of comfort into his ears as he struggled to get his words out.

'It's pure f-fuckery, yuh know? All of us there, saying how sorry *we* are, like this just happen naturally. Looking each other in the *eye* –' He spat the word out in disgust, emphasising the extra 'y' his dialect placed in front of the word when he was angry. '– pretending this what we signed up for when we came here. This . . . fucking—'

'Yuh wan Mikey fi hear yuh?' warned Mikey's mother, glancing at the door where the boy was lingering.

Mikey pulled back his head. His father's anger and his mother's shame made him feel uncomfortable. Like he shouldn't be watching. He shouldn't know his father's nose ran when he cried, that his eyes went red and the bags underneath them puffed up, making his already slight eyes look even smaller. But he didn't stop. This was grown people's business, but he couldn't help but be moved by the truth of that privacy. Almost like that time he'd walked in on them ... doing whatever they were doing when they thought they had the house to themselves one Sunday afternoon.

His father was still going. 'The pickney dem cyaan even pay their respect, because wah? Dem white boys might lick dem off too? And yet, we stay. Scraping together scraps to do wah with? Mi never come here fi survive and survive only.'

Mikey's mother placed the tips of her delicate umber fingers underneath his chin and raised his head from her left shoulder. They both looked at the wet patch his tears and snot had left behind on her black blouse and burst into laughter.

'See how you crease up the supmn, suh?' Mikey's mother kissed her teeth playfully. 'We're not going to be here forever. Okay? I know you're worried but *believe* me. Please.'

Mikey's father nodded. For the first time since he'd arrived in London, Mikey realised how skilled both his parents were at lying; to him, to each other, to themselves.

Chapter Two: The Flight

(Harmondsworth, 2012)

Frank woke up that morning knowing he might never see his family in one place again. He was oddly calm. Numb, but with the dazed determination of a commuter at 8 a.m. He dutifully swung his muscular legs out from under the sheets, gingerly placed his dry, bare feet on the cool linoleum and let out a yawn. He was glad to be leaving this room, his roommate, this place. While he knew he'd find it harder to depart from England, the country he'd called home for over thirty years, he was preoccupied with what his family would say when he told them, finally, that the fight was over. With just hours before his flight, he hadn't managed to break it to them just yet. But not for want of trying.

'We're going to beat this, Daddy,' his daughter Charmaine assured him on her last visit. He knew she didn't believe it. It had been months of the same thing, over and over. Jamaican and British High Commission visits, intended, they told him, to 'establish his identity'. But if not Frank Brown, son of Gloria and Percy Brown, proud East Londoner since the age of twelve, then who was he? Who did these authorities want him to be so badly? Why had they been on his case ever since that police officer stopped him in his car that Thursday?

Frank rose and wiped the crust from his eyes. Even with limited grooming tools, he was still noticeably handsome. His hair had grown out into a shapeless short afro. It needed combing – not the coping method he'd adopted over the past few years: picking at it, twisting it, pulling it out. His sharp cheekbones still glowed in the fluorescent light, the dingy, yellow tinge in his room highlighting his freckled brown skin and deep brown eyes. His body was still impressive. The muscles on his arms had definition. His six-pack had long faded, but firm pecs remained. He was tall, in that charmingly awkward way. At forty-nine, he looked thirty-five. A blessing that had landed him with several children over the years, and one or two babymothers who remained infatuated. His children thought nobody could hold a candle to him too. They defended him when he made mistakes. They were still staunchly defending him now, he thought. I *seem* nice, he said to himself. But I must not be if this keeps happening.

It was easier to blame himself. There was no other person he could point towards. The image of the face of the woman who first told him his immigration status was being called into question sent chills down his back, but she was just a messenger. Not the judge who told him weeks earlier that his kids no longer needed him, wouldn't miss him with almost 5,000 miles between them. Not the Border Agency, or the Home Office, or the Prime Minister. Though they were all fucking bastards, the judge especially. Sometimes picturing his miserable face stunned into silence after an imaginary cussing out, delivered by Frank himself, was enough to placate him. But not for long. His mother had warned him when he struggled during those first British years after arriving from Saint Catherine, Jamaica, that if he had focused he might have made more of himself. Frank was starting to believe it too.

He took two steps towards the weighted bouquet of white and pink daisies, roses, Peruvian lilies and white snapdragon by his bed, and took in the scent. He stopped, picked up the flowers and did it again. A decaying lily leaf fell away from the bunch and landed on the floor. The flowers had died about two weeks ago. There was no longer a natural perfume to take away the faint stench of stale sweat, piss and cleaning products. But it was the only beautiful thing here and the act of sniffing tricked him into enjoying it. Charmaine and Shelly, his first two children, had spent more on those flowers than they should have to make him happy. He was going to get everything out of them. Even as they crumbled into dust.

The buckle of the aeroplane seatbelt felt ice cold in Frank's hands. He could feel his heart beating out of his chest. He had known the phone calls half an hour before take-off would be too much to process, both for him and Charmaine, the last of the kids to know. He placed the clip into the slot and heard it click as the flight attendants grappled with fussy passengers and oversized luggage. It was happening. After years of wading through life's choppy waters, he'd finally been swallowed up by a tsunami. He had given this country his best. It had washed it all away without apology.

Frank removed his smartphone, a cracked Samsung he hadn't seen since he was out for a short spell the year before, from his pocket. He had dozens of missed calls. But his thoughts went to the day he cracked the phone, his mind eager to be anywhere but here. He had been dancing at the afterparty for his granddaughter's christening. It was a risky move, his old signature, a dipping and hip-gyrating three-step routine that without fail made him the centre of attention on any dancefloor. This time, his broken screen, and not his rubber waistline, did it. He cracked a half-hearted smile thinking about it. It would be easy to distract himself with the memory of the time spent with his family and friends last year, after three years in detention. But even that period had been fraught with worry and uncertainty. No, he was doing the right thing by leaving. He knew he would crack – like so many others in Colnbrook already had – if he didn't. Besides, now that the Home Office was aware of his intention to leave, there wasn't much more he could do to stop it.

He swiped up on the just about functional phone, narrowly avoiding a nasty gash when a stray piece of glass brushed against his thumb. All he had to do was press call on the last number that had tried him, Charmaine's. He found himself lingering instead. What would his daughter think of his decision to give up? Would she blame him? He hoped not. She'd always been the most compassionate and level-headed of his children. Even throughout the divorce from her and Shelly's mother. Now, her reaction was less certain. He didn't want to hear her cry like his mother had an hour ago. Or to hang up on him, like his second ex-partner, Ruth, had. Frank dialled and held the phone an inch away from his ear.

'H-hello?' whispered Charmaine's strained voice on the other end. He could tell someone had broken the news to her already. She sounded as if she had been crying, screaming, and shouting for the entire world, and had only just stopped for breath.

'Charmaine . . .' he said.

'H-hello?'

'Charmaine, I'm . . .' Frank took a deep breath and stared at the seatbelt sign above him to stop from crying. '. . . sorry.'

'And you're leaving n-now?'

Frank bit his lip so hard he drew blood. 'Yes.'

'Okay . . . okay . . . fuck!'

'*Charmaine!*' Her swearing had thrown him a bone. He could focus on that, as if it mattered, instead of her agonised wailing. Anything, anything but that.

'Sorry, Daddy. I just . . . I can't believe this is happening. I thought we'd have more time. I thought—'

'Yuh talk like mi dead, darling. I'll see you soon, yuh ear? This ting nuh over yet. Not while I'm around. We've just had to take . . . a weh dem call it . . . a likkle . . . *detour,* that's all. Besides, you always said you thought life would be better back home. I suppose I'll just have to find out.'

Charmaine made a noise that Frank knew was meant to be a giggle. But she was still crying. Talking to him like this was hurting her. He didn't want to do it any more.

'Listen, Dad. Just run me through everything right now, okay? I know this is hard for you, but I need to know so we can win this thing and get you back. Who are you staying with? How will you make any money? Is this voluntary?'

'Excuse me, sir, I'm so sorry but you'll have to end your call and put your phone on flight mode now. We're getting ready to depart,' said a snippy flight attendant who was leaning over the empty seat next to Frank to get his attention. He had been repeating himself for the past couple of minutes, but Frank had insisted on ignoring the coiffed young man's flatly polite requests. He needed an enemy on his flight. The attendant's patronising tone made him an easy target. He knew he was projecting, but he needed to. Frank raised a single finger, then a prayer gesture, hoping the gestures would buy him thirty more seconds.

'Remember I told you about that place in Negril? Mi friend Mongoose have a guest house I can stay at for a likkle while. Maybe some work too. I'll be fine, honest.' Frank was lying, but it was helping. He carried on.

'When mi reach, the embassy did seh dem 'elp appeal mi case, so it's all a matter of when now, not if.' More lies.

'You really, really, don't have to worry.'

'Sir, please switch off your phone.'

'Mi already tell you, ONE SECOND. Mi cyaan have ONE second to say goodbye to mi daughter?'

The attendant massaged his tanned right temple with his middle and index fingers and used his other hand to gesture to Frank that if he didn't wrap it up soon, there would be trouble.

'You have to go,' said Charmaine.

'I have to go … yes. Listen, I love you. I love all of you. Please don't be sad.'

'I know you love me, Daddy. And I love you too … I'm so, so sorry.'

He went silent. What could he say in response to something so heart-breaking?

'Goodbye, Charmaine, speak tomorrow, okay?'

'Okay. Buh-bye.'

Frank felt the blood in his veins turning to ice. He slowly lowered the hand that was gripping the phone and whispered 'wow'. The flight attendant smiled at him and turned to resume his duties. They were taking off now. But the sinking feeling in the pit of his stomach had nothing to do with the plane. Turning to get what he was sure was his last glance at Greater London, he cosied up to the window and stared down as the ground moved further and further away.

What now? he thought.

Chapter Three: The Arrival

(Tottenham, 2007)

Judith had been trying to hide her disappointment for two hours. Her face was beginning to hurt. The pained smile felt like a bruise. She wore it anyway.

When Lisa pulled onto the narrow street full of terraced houses, Judith beamed. As she stepped out of the car and into the damp sleet that had blanketed the city for the past day or so, she squealed 'wee!' in place of cussing. When they walked through the splintered, paint-chipped door with all those locks into a cramped, piss-stinking space between the two flats, she feigned excitement. *An apartment? Even less space for me? God bless this country*, she thought sarcastically.

'This is it,' Lisa said as they entered the second-floor flat, Judith trailing behind her, stealing looks at her cropped hair and cocky walk. Excluding her fashion sense – denim jeans and a too-tight rhinestoned tank top – her cousin still carried the air of what they accused her of back home. She still wondered whether the rumours were true. The door opened to a dark corridor with six closed doors running along either side. It was overdue a splash of paint. The stippled, yellowing wallpaper made her feel uneasy. Clusters and raised bumps, like scabs. *Horrible*. She followed her cousin past the other rooms to the end of the walkway. Something crashed. A high-pitched voice squealed. There was a child here too.

'Three years old. Nasty age,' said Lisa, as she struggled with the key. Judith didn't know Lisa had a child. Why hadn't she mentioned it? Perhaps she wasn't *that* way inclined after all.

'She's not mine! She's . . .' said Lisa, sensing suspicions. She gestured at the off-white door down the end of the hallway. Judith enjoyed kids. She liked it just as much when they had other homes to go to.

'. . . I don't think he's in. Come inside.'

'He?'

Lisa ignored her cousin and pushed against the door in front of them. It opened with a cartoonish creak. The six-foot by nine-foot room was as bare as the corridor, save for a metal bunk bed with an empty futon frame underneath. The single thrill was a net curtain on the sash window, with rot around the edges of the window frame. The wooden floor was coming up. Judith didn't want to touch anything.

'I know, I know. The good news is I have a spare mattress for you. I just need to pick it up. The bad news is, we're sharing tonight.' Lisa didn't look her in the eye. She hadn't since they got in the beat-up car at Heathrow.

'Nuh budda look pon mi vehicle, it'll get us where we need to go,' she'd said in jest, laughing a little too hard, her accent much thinner and patois less natural than Judith remembered years before. At fifty-four, Lisa was a good twenty-seven years younger than her, after all. It made sense that aspects of her speech had already begun adapting to this place a few years after her arrival. The same little girl who'd fled without so much as a couple of months' warning all those years ago. Just older and more British. Judith was taking it all in. The cold, the people, the ugliness. The implausibility that this place could ever truly feel like home.

When Lisa left Jamaica for London after the incident that drove her across oceans, Judith knew her cousin hadn't found it as nice as described, despite her cheery front on the phone and light stories of how the 'British people dem gwan'. But she'd no idea it would be as bleak as this. Whose kid had she heard screaming? How many other adults were in this place? Where was the kitchen? Were they allowed to use it? How did Lisa end up here? Judith stumbled backwards, hitting the metal frame meant for a futon next to her, questions racing.

'Judith!' Lisa looked at her cousin in the eye for the first time in hours. Humour had broken the tension. She was trying, desperately, not to let out a snort at Judith's slapstick stumble backwards. Judith cut her eye at Lisa. There was something irritating about her cousin's amusement. Look at where they were. Look at what she was sitting on.

'Eee-hee, laugh yuh ah laugh,' Judith muttered under her breath, stroking her hands across the metallic, cushion-less frame as she doggedly refused to return her cousin's gaze.

'Don't be like that.'

Judith pushed her lips upwards and raised her eyebrows to say: 'Yeah, whatever.' A juvenile response, she knew. But she wanted Lisa to get it without having to spell it out: what were they doing calling this place a home?

Lisa circled the futon frame and perched on the edge of the curved wooden desk built into the bunk. She had to bend her neck to sit down, the beams creaking under her weight.

'Let me guess: you have a whole heap of questions for me,' said Lisa.

Judith raised an eyebrow. The blasé tone her cousin was affecting wasn't fooling anyone. It was strange they hadn't addressed the elephant in the room yet. That they were sitting here quietly, in a room that could barely contain either of them, with nothing for a view but a crumbling, moss-infested wall directly opposite and the hanging threat of roommates she hadn't even met yet. Judith considered maintaining silence; the burden of coming clean didn't rest on her shoulders. But Lisa's forced, wavering smirk made her melt. She could feel her cousin's shame.

'So, what do you think?' Lisa said, turning with her arms outstretched as if she were in grand surroundings.

'Lisa . . .' said Judith, willing honesty from her cousin with her stare. Lisa looked down instead. Judith repeated her name again.

'What?' said Lisa, trying to keep the air light. Judith raised an eyebrow.

'Yuh know seh mi nah 'fraid fi be honest. But nuh botha ask *me* "what do ya think?"' Judith said, mocking her cousin's accent. 'Mi wan ear your truth. What do *you* think?'

'Me?' Lisa clutched her chest.

'No, the cat's mother.'

Judith met Lisa's gaze once more, hoping she wouldn't have to spell it out, for both their sakes. She outstretched her hand, gesturing for Lisa to do the same. As their fingertips brushed against one another's, Lisa's body crumbled slightly, broken and saved by the contact. She exhaled, still looking at Judith. The wooden slats continued to creak.

'That wood cyaan hold yuh, cuz,' Judith offered, smiling softly, knowing Lisa wasn't ready to spill just yet.

Lisa kissed her teeth and stifled a chuckle as she rose from her seat to sit by the gap on the floor between the futon and the desk. She was still holding Judith's hand, but tighter now.

'You see how your cuz get fat?' she said, slapping her fleshy gut, not quite convincing herself of her feigned brightness.

'I ... guess I'll start from the top then ... you got a few hours?' She laughed.

As Lisa's reality became marginally clearer, Judith felt heavier. She reeled as Lisa offered sparse details about their subletting landlord, Delroy, who used the place as his pad but didn't actually live there full time. About Shirley, the mother of the screaming child. And vaguely, about her place in all this – short of how she made money.

'He isn't here all the time. And when he is, you won't have to deal with him. It's just, he's helpful to have around when ... he helps with ...' Lisa looked away, unsure as to whether the whole truth was the best medicine for her homesick, jet-lagged cousin.

'Never mind all that now. *Delroy* isn't here,' Lisa whispered his name when she said it, a diminuendo of: *Delroy, delroy, del-roy*. Why? wondered Judith.

'Him nah 'ere?'

Lisa shook her head.

'So, if him gaan, then why are you talking like that?'

'It's nothing!' Lisa said, louder than she'd meant to. She bent her head downwards. When she brought it up again, there was a false pep in her face and voice that gave away the game. She knew it, Judith knew it. But she carried on.

'You know how *inna* some people can be,' she said with
a tinge of desperation. 'I'm being careful. They do talk, and
she is in there.'

'So, they're a couple?' said Judith.

'Sometimes.'

'Weh yuh mean?'

'She's his babymother, but as far as couple-couple? I don't
know.'

'Ah wah "couple-couple"?'

'Like, they're a family . . . technically. But are they in love?
Or even *like*?' Lisa was whispering again.

'But him sleep here—'

'—sometimes,' Lisa interrupted.

'What about the woman? Shirley?'

'Shh, say their names *quietly*.'

'An' she just *fine* with it, suh? Just a smile when him say
him ready?'

Lisa nodded.

'Bwoi,' Judith said, heavily. There was more to it, but she
didn't want to push too hard. 'You're not scared of him, are
you?' she added, a part of her hoping Lisa wouldn't answer
either way. She already had by swallowing and looking at the
floor. Whether Lisa came out with it or not, Judith could only
imagine what she'd had to deal with if he was as bullying as he
sounded. Trying her best to drown out the ranting she could
now hear down the hall – the slurred ramblings of a man who
had a song on his heart and too much to drink – Judith got
up and hugged Lisa tightly.

'Is that him?'

Lisa nodded and gently pushed her away, patting her on the

back. Judith nodded back, the only sign of reassurance she could think to offer. They'd never met, but she felt a chill on hearing the bass in that man's muffled voice.

'Yuh nuh haffi to tell me everything now. But we're *family*. We haffi look out for each other, y'hear?' she said, embracing her cousin.

Lisa wasn't going to come clean now. But when she did, whatever it was she was avoiding would be bad. Judith changed the subject.

'Mi just fly how many thousand miles across the worl, and mi nah get no food or likkle drink fi quench mi thirst. Cha,' Judith offered as a distraction.

Lisa smiled for real this time.

'Go check the stove in the kitchen. It's to your left, the white door.' Judith dutifully followed her cousin's instructions and left the room, hoping she wouldn't run into either of those strangers in the hallway.

'Cups and plates in the cupboard next to the sink, drinks in the fridge, and you can't miss the microwave!' Lisa shouted after her. This was it, she thought. Another piece in the puzzle that her family thought was her life slotting into place. There'd be no more hiding now. And not for the first time.

It took just a few months for Judith to work out the best means of saving money in what she'd begun to call 'Teefing London'. The supermarkets she could just about afford for bulk items; the markets, grocers, fishmongers and butchers with the best deals and a willingness to let her haggle; the dishes she froze each Sunday for the coming weeks and, sometimes, the food banks. But this was a special occasion. Not a happy one, but worth attempting to remedy with food.

After a night of listening to Shirley's chilling screams and the dull thuds that refused to stop landing against what sounded like her bones, Judith needed to give at least one person in that flat something else to think about. Since she'd begun her health and social care studies in college, the basis of her visa, she'd kept to herself. She felt, despite hearing Jamaican accents in abundance in the city, like she stood out. Like everyone could see her foreignness on her.

Isolation was a shield and a sanction that she felt she had no choice but to cling to. Getting to know her coursemates, a varied group of largely Black, brown and European women who all seemed to be there to make friends, not focus on what they were learning, seemed pointless. She'd eat lunch alone and watch them grow closer, only occasionally letting herself wonder whether she should join them too. Her pride would not let her do it. England had brought out of her a stone-cold disposition, keeping people at bay by design.

The women in her home, however, she could not afford to ice out entirely. Not when she heard the things she heard, saw the things she saw. Her secretive, untamed cousin tested her patience – but she was family. And Shirley was a mother, a woman, no matter how annoying she was, or how often she cursed and belched for attention. She decided to cook for them. It wouldn't remedy much else but mild hunger on a Saturday evening, but even that seemed to count for a lot in this house. Lisa's and Shirley's culinary skills were largely confined to opening packages and jamming buttons on the microwave. Delroy's were non-existent – and yet more evidence of what sort of man he was. Her father, uncles and cousins back home at least knew how to feed themselves. Some better cooks than the women in her family. Not here.

Judith's fragrant stews, soups and curries, therefore, didn't last very long. Though she'd never seen Shirley or Delroy help themselves, crumbs, polished bones in the bin and spoons soiled with viscous liquid gave away how frequently they'd dip in. She knew how coveted her meals were in this household. The meat – thick, plentiful pieces of mutton – would be for later. The rest was for the late breakfast she was planning on making: saltfish fritters with ackee (scrambled egg for Shirley – she didn't like all that 'weird yellow stuff, like. No offence') pear, or what the people here called 'avocado', and fried plantain on the side. Conversation may not have always been in Judith's wheelhouse in that household, but in the love-language of food she was silver-tongued.

Shirley had grown up around Caribbeans in northwest London, gyrated her body to familiar rhythms from the region, procured burned CDs of dancehall artists like Sizzla, Capleton, Sean Paul and Wayne Wonder, and picked up slang that quietly irked her northern mother. As a teen, she'd worn her mousy-brown straight hair gelled onto her forehead in a swooping fringe, the rest back-combed into a high, slick bun, creating volume that her hair texture ordinarily wouldn't allow.

She'd chalked it up to remaining close friends with her neighbours, a group of largely Black Caribbean and West African girls and boys she played out with before her mother got home from work. Her humour and ease around them had enamoured her to them. She'd got cosy enough to know their families, the aromas of their food – that she would politely decline with the lie that 'Mum's cooked, sorry' – even take some pride in the labels her white peers would give her at school, like 'wigga', or 'reverse Oreo'. It wasn't until she became a teenager that she intentionally immersed herself in the community that she felt loved her as much as she loved it.

'You should do comedy,' her friends would tell her whenever she delivered a witty quip, leaving them wheezing and clutching their stomachs. What was received with detentions and pursed lips from the uptight teachers at her school made her somewhat of a star in these circles. She'd never had so much positive attention. At home, her need for an audience was more often met with exasperation. Her mother, weary from working multiple cleaning shifts, too deep in her own worries to come up for air. The praise would invoke in her daydreams of an adult version of herself, cocky and loose-limbed in a dark room, unfazed by blinding stage lights, giving it to a crowd of faceless, doubled-over adorers. She was sure that sense of assurance was how, once she'd turned eighteen, she'd sailed happily enough through shifts at the local bookies for five years, her audience a horde of mostly drunken, leering or lonely men, but just as tickled as her neighbours had once been. Her boss Martin was her number-one fan. Mesmerised by her confidence and wit, she could feel his eyes on her whenever she gave as good as she got. He adored her for it. The punters came around to respect her for it.

Shirley had no relationship with her father, a man she barely remembered save for the sound of his keys in the door in the early hours of the morning, muffled shouting through the paper-thin walls of her bedroom or the punched holes he'd left permanently impressed in the white, varnished doors of her mother's flat. His absence, prolonged since she turned twelve, wasn't a balm in itself, either. She'd clash with her mother daily, frustrated with her fixation on money, what Shirley wore, 'those people' she hung around with, and her charade about why it was important to do well in school. Rich, she thought, coming from someone who'd dropped out herself at fifteen after falling pregnant with Shirley during a weekend of partying with her then twenty-five-year-old father in London. For all her motherly behaviour – the nagging, being nosy, the bossiness – she felt to Shirley like an annoying older sister with the short few years between them. The last thing Shirley wanted was to end up like her. Finding people, music, clothing that felt like the furthest thing from that image seemed like the easiest way to make that distinction clear.

Shirley's first boyfriend, a Grenadian DJ called David, was her first physical escape from the snot-nosed screaming matches and door-slamming. They'd met at an 18+ rave in Tottenham that she and her friends had managed to sneak into aged sixteen. Armed with Alizé's liquid courage, she'd swung her hips all the way to the DJ booth, her all-white, knock-off Juicy Couture velour tracksuit, with a revealing pink vest top underneath, turning his head while he spun the decks. He had a face and body that his cockiness made more appealing: lanky, slim, a little rat-faced, with acne scars dotted around on his dark brown skin. He looked younger than his twenty-one years, but seemed a much older and wiser man to Shirley. She stayed over at his flat in Walthamstow that night and never went home, moving, when the thing with David ended, to another flat with another man, from flat to flat, one relationship after another – until she met Delroy.

Through all that, Caribbean food was still a mystery to her. Something to begrudgingly snack on when offered, but never something she chose intentionally to eat. For all her eagerness to distance herself from anything related to her mother, she still had her taste for English comfort food. Until, behind Judith's back one evening, out of spite for being slighted, she stuck a finger, then the tip of a knife, and then a tablespoon, into a curry her housemate had left steaming on the stove. She was seduced. It started with the acceptance of offerings of festivals – sweet, fried cornmeal dumplings. A crumb of sweet gizzada here and there. The clincher was a small piece of brown stew chicken she'd been able to steal from the large Dutch pot on the stove when Judith wasn't looking one evening. Her body melted as the flavours spread over her tongue. Her manner towards Judith would take longer to thaw.

These days, Shirley's wit and charm had about as much effect on her housemates as a child bashing Lego bricks together. Delroy only found her funny when he was drunk, or wanted something, or when their daughter was watching. Lisa's tittering, though frequent, was laced with sympathy. It hadn't rubbed off on her cousin. She'd dart her eyes to the side when Shirley spoke, hum hymns when Shirley was mid-speech, or walk out of the room seconds after she'd entered. After the unsettling events the night before, she was sure she'd get more judgement from the woman. She wasn't sure she could handle it without giving her a piece of her mind.

Who does she think she is? Shirley thought, as she caressed the violet-black bruise on her wrist, trying not to agitate more pain. They were all living in this shithole together. And that woman was sharing a room with her little cousin, yet still had the nerve to be stoosh. Shirley kissed her teeth. But even that hurt. She could still feel Delroy wrapped around her, his eyes burning into hers as he gripped tighter, accusing her of things she had and hadn't done, throwing Martin's name like a grenade. Gathering herself, she took a seat by the chest by her bedroom window and lit up a cigarette. Her and Lisa, the ones who held up the majority of the rent, judged by a mature student who was paid minimum wage and had no life. Ridiculous. But even as she watched the embers of the fag give way to ash, terrified at the thought of Delroy returning home, a part of her still wanted approval. Craning her neck to get a glimpse of the street below, she spotted Judith in the distance, struggling to bring her bags home. She blew out the last puff of smoke before she flicked her cigarette butt onto the pavement below and wondered: *Why do I care so much?*

When she made it back onto the street, Judith took her time. Though her bags were heavy, she didn't want a chance encounter with Delroy, whose habit was to overcompensate with small talk each time he'd finished slapping up Shirley. It had happened three times now. In three months. He'd find a way to corner her outside, apologising for the noise and his woman's drama, despite him being a man of peace.

Judith placed her bags against the crumbling wall of the abandoned hall at the end of her street. Though its windows had been punctured, the foundations wasting away with each passing year, the foliage looked almost manicured, in that beautiful way plants tend to when they're left undisturbed by humans. Winding and elaborate, it snaked through bricks and over windowpanes, around what used to be the front door and into the cavernous jungle inside. Lisa had told Judith it had been a church a few years ago, and a youth centre before that. Shame. Must've been nice, thought Judith, who had to travel a full hour to get to the church of her choice: St John's in Haringey. Looking at it now, as the weight of the mood at home crept back onto her shoulders, it felt like a damn travesty. She wanted to tend to the vines and cherry blossoms and ivy. Fashion it into some kind of paradise, and use the building to cleanse her spirit, and Shirley's and especially Delroy's and maybe Lisa's too, while she was at it. She looked down at her watch. 10.23 a.m. She'd better get back if she was going to make that precious time slot Shirley had convinced herself was the peak of daytime dining: brunch.

When she got to the door of their flat, she spotted the top of Shirley's head in her bedroom window, her blonde ponytail bobbing around as she failed to duck her head out of view. Shirley would have gone unnoticed had the timing been a fraction of a second more in her favour. Conceding defeat, she let out a too-chipper-to-not-be-masking-pain 'Hiya love! Oh gosh, your back must be *killing*. I'll come down and help you with the bags, yeah?' and disappeared out of view. Even from that height, Judith could see it, the bruising. In some patches, the redness had already begun to darken to a deep blue, her eye puffy and tender-looking, looking as if it was barely able to withstand a brush of a finger. Judith felt a pang of coldness in her chest, as if she could feel the soreness. She thanked God Shirley's daughter had been at her grandmother's this weekend, but wasn't sure it would've changed things if she hadn't been.

The door cracked open just enough for Shirley to poke her good eye, the right one, out of it.

'Oooh! *Someone's* been busy,' said Shirley, bending her head as low as she could as she attempted to take one of the carrier bags from the doorstep. She'd barely lifted one before she doubled over in pain.

'Go back upstairs,' Judith said, colder than she'd meant to.

'No, really. Let me—'

Judith looked Shirley in the eyes and tilted her head forward. Without responding, Shirley dutifully turned around and began to climb the stairs, maintaining the charade as best she could as she tried to change the subject and mask the pain of lifting her bruised body up each step.

'You're proper . . .' Shirley stopped herself.

Taking the bait, Judith chimed in.

'Mi propa . . . what?'

'Nothing,' said Shirley, continuing hesitantly up the stairs, trying to think of the right thing to say to win this woman round.

'No I was just—' she turned around to face Judith, biting her lip like a nervous child, while Judith stared back blankly and unimpressed.

'I was gonna say. You're, you know, independent, aren't you?'

'Wah mek yuh say dat?' Judith puffed, stifling a laugh as she struggled into the doorway of the flat with the bags, wary of this white woman's flirtation with cliches about Black women.

Shirley chuckled.

'I've noticed and I like it. That's all.'

Judith ignored her and unpacked the food. Shirley just needed to talk, even if she wasn't saying much of anything. If that meant having to take what felt like forced compliments, she would, in the most nonchalant way possible. But she wouldn't entertain them. Shirley stood behind her – almost a little too close – as she prepared the meal. Asked questions when she missed a step in the recipe she'd noted down the last time Judith made saltfish fritters, her gaze just a tad too intense for the atmosphere to be anything but a little uncomfortable.

Judith's saltfish fritters:

Remove the saltfish from the pot, drain it, and boil it again *ask Judith how many times

Dice onions and garlic; dice scotch bonnet peppers *note to self, maybe not a whole one … and wear gloves … and remove the seeds, too*; sprinkle in some of those herbs *Judith says it's thyme* and chuck them into a bowl of plain flour

Add water to the flour *ask Judith how much later. Missed that bit, wasn't looking* and mix it all in together.

Remove the saltfish from the boil again and crumble the flakes of saltfish into the dough, along with that orange seasoning she's always using, and a bit of olive oil

Shape the dough into little discs *like a little mini pancake* and fry on each side until a bit golden brown

'So, your daughter's stopping with her grandmother?' Judith said as she scraped scrambled eggs from the skillet and onto Shirley's plate, where the rest of the food was resting. Shirley nodded.

'Yeah, I'm sure she's nyaming everything in sight, driving my mum mad.'

'Like mother, like daughter,' Judith muttered, wondering if she'd gone too far.

'Cheeky . . . I mean, you're not wrong.' Shirley guffawed, taking an eager a bite of the food before her.

'Judith, oh my god. This is *buff*,' she said between mouthfuls of saltfish fritters, scrambled eggs, avocado and grilled cherry tomatoes. She accompanied each bite with a large gulp of lukewarm tea and a bite of hardo bread, spooning the food into her mouth with such fervour that Judith wondered whether her hunger had been building up for some days.

'How's your . . .' Judith gestured towards Shirley's eye, then busied herself with wiping non-existent debris off one of the kitchen countertops.

Shirley nodded and wiped her mouth, pushing her plate away from the edge of the table, as if it too needed to be protected from the reality of her situation.

'I don't think anything's broken this time,' she said. 'Which is progress for D,' she spluttered, still chewing the mouthful of bread she'd taken a bite of. Judith didn't say anything. She didn't know how to in that moment. Shirley smiled at her as if to say 'it's okay', and continued to eat.

'Well . . . it cyaan . . . it cyaan go on for much longer. There has to be . . . something . . .' she trailed off.

'Judith. It can, and there's nothing.'

'You could leave,' said Judith without thinking. Shirley burst into laughter.

'You think I haven't tried that before?'

Silence of what felt like hours passed between them, the seeming inevitability of the situation a cruel joke that Judith didn't quite get and didn't want to.

Shirley took Judith's hand and pulled her closer.

'You did the right thing, picking up that catering job as soon as you could. Getting your own little money and that. But trust, Judith, this place is full of surprises. Sometimes those companies stop calling. Sometimes those salaries don't cut it. And that's when you have to do whatever you can to make things happen. It's all work, at the end of the day, isn't it?'

Judith resented the air of condescension Shirley appeared to be adopting. That she, a big woman of almost fifty, who'd flown far away from the home and people she loved, the hopes and expectations of her family a load on her back, didn't understand what sacrifice looked like. What it pushed you towards. The 'little money' she was earning was going to that wutless babyfather of Shirley's, to her mother at home, to her sister, her sister's kids, her cousins, their kids. It was going into this white woman's mouth in this very moment. She wasn't going to be shamed about doing things that Shirley thought were beneath her.

Though they had never discussed exactly what 'work' Delroy kept putting Lisa and Shirley up to, which friends of his they had gone to see, or where they'd stay when these visits spanned twenty-four hours – or longer – Judith knew now exactly what Shirley – and Lisa too, apparently – thought a worthy sacrifice. She couldn't bring herself to engage. She began clearing up the plates.

'Look, I'm not saying it's for everyone. I don't even know if it's for me.'

Judith averted her eyes and began to hum the Grace Thrillers' 'Living Waters' under her breath as she wiped down the surfaces of the countertops, her attempt to lose herself in the righteous lyrics failing as Shirley blathered on in the background. What worked for this woman was fine for her, if that's what she truly wanted for herself. But it wasn't what Judith wanted for her cousin. Wasn't what she wanted to be around. Or think of as normal. It wasn't right.

This godless place was trying to turn her. She didn't want to let it. Delroy may have been able to bully Shirley and Lisa into submission, but she'd die before she let that happen to her. Her thoughts turned to Shirley's daughter Megan. That poor child. What was her place in all of this? What sort of example were Shirley and Delroy setting? She wasn't sure she could stomach living here now she knew what was really going on. That man and his mood swings and his fists, and his stinking bile breath, his sporadic demands for extra cash for the 'rent', or a chance to remind the women how dependent they were on him, were a cancer. She hummed harder and fixated on the dilapidated building in view from the kitchen window, the force of her melodic murmuring hurting the back of her throat. Shirley placed a hand on her arm from behind.

'It's okay. We don't have to talk about this,' she said.

Judith paused her vigorous scrubbing and sighed towards the heavens. Perhaps she was being too harsh on the woman.

'Yuh don't have to . . . there are other ways to make money,' she said, hoping to change Shirley's mind. Somehow. Needing her to.

'Judith,' said Shirley, conceding defeat. Perhaps it was best to stop talking about this after all. Judith turned around and looked the woman in the eyes. She felt hopeless.

'Every day, the devil helps the teef,' Judith said to a perplexed Shirley, who took a second or two to realise that this was the start of another of her famous sayings that she didn't quite understand. 'One day? God will help the watchman, y'hear?' she continued, the message sinking in a little. Shirley grinned and caressed Judith's stray hand, catching her by surprise. The two women smiled at each other, neither of them aware of Lisa's lingering presence in the doorway.

Chapter Four: The Dance

(Notting Hill, 1963)

The music from the restaurant downstairs always seemed to boom louder when he knew he couldn't enjoy it. Mikey loved a good shebeen, but not when it meant working for his parents all night, dodging drunken punters, balancing hot food and dirty plates. He was on duty; there'd be no fun, he understood. It was what his father had said the first time his parents ordered his assistance at their monthly dance, an event that had evolved after years of smaller gatherings with their closest friends, where dominoes were slammed down with force and the rum punch kept flowing.

'And nuh botha teef nuh food okay? I counted every last patty yuh motha prepare,' his father added, rather unnecessarily, Mikey thought. A few years ago, yes, he couldn't help himself. He'd swipe meat from Dutch pots or break off corners of flaky, golden-yellow patty pastry without thought. He usually left behind a trail of crumbs or gravy stains, guaranteeing a beating later. Not now. He knew better than to leave evidence.

These days, his parents' party had become a larger affair, a crowd made up mostly of London-based West Indians, with a dusting of visitors and plus ones from up north or Europe. The furniture was rearranged to accommodate the bustling crowds, the chequered tiles pointlessly swept and polished to even higher standards than usual. Whereas before, Mikey could get away with simply greeting his parents' friends, passing out trays of food for an hour or so, or bashfully performing at some elders' request before slipping away, he had no such option now. Hiding in the flat with an image in his mind and a pen and pencil to realise it was out of the question these days. He wished he could be out with friends, trying his luck with the girls who would find his awkwardness mysterious, his preoccupation with art and politics, though verging on pretentiousness, just as alluring as it was meant to seem intimidating. Good-looking as Mikey was becoming as a young man, it was those traits that gave him an edge. He had first realised this at the last party he'd been to, when Tina McDonald pushed her fingers through her bountiful curls, staring right into his eyes from across the circle where he was holding court. She was the prettiest girl in the room. He'd been complaining about the Commonwealth Immigrants Act, a rant copied near word for word from his father. She'd been listening intently, fluttering her grey eyes as his impassioned speech grew more intense.

To everyone else in the dim of the family restaurant, this was one of the best parties you could find – the crowd as lively as anywhere, the men as eager and boisterous, the girls as pretty and confident. That Mikey came as a package with his parents, even at the age of eighteen, had no bearing on anyone but him. Empty glasses were passed to him with a pat on his springy afro, enquiries about the food – and did your daddy make any more of his famous brown stew chicken? – rolled in by the minute. Had his parents made a deal with every guest and gatecrasher to ensure that their son was to have no fun under any circumstances? It felt possible. With resignation, he accepted his place and took one of few seats in the room by the candy-red Formica table in the corner of the main room of the restaurant.

It was a lengthy yet poky space, even with most of its furniture crammed in their living room upstairs. Mikey had parked himself at the designated spot for plates of bones and leftovers and abandoned drinks. The only other place to sit was on the sole bench opposite the DJ – and all the elders, and shy boys and girls, had staked their claim on that area hours ago. Mikey glanced around the room, longing, for a second, to be a part of the fun his parents curated each month. The pulsating bass pounded off the chests of gyrating bodies, twisting faces into laughter and deep satisfaction with each skip of the ska beat. Women's eyes moved seductively across their own bodies as they traced geometric shapes with their wire waists. Men, some stationed behind women, gave as good as they got, pelting their hips to match the rhythm of their dance partners, and bending their rubber knees with ease. *This* was what rubbing off wallpaper looked like. And though he knew he couldn't take part without guaranteed interruption, it didn't stop him from moving his behind in his seat as grains of discarded rice jumped in unison with the bass.

'Enjoying the music there, champ?' a deep voice with an accent Mikey couldn't quite place said from nowhere. Mikey looked up to see the thick, protruding torso of a young, sharp-suited man standing right in front of him. The man's face, a kind, dark-skinned, acne-scarred face, softened into a smile, flashing white teeth and pillowy lips. He looked like an authority of some kind, like an old film-noir detective, the brim of his fedora leaving one glinting eye exposed, and his voice sounded . . . twangy. But in a non-West Indian way. More like a cowboy or something. An *American*.

Mikey looked up into the man's eyes for a couple of seconds, inspecting the worn leather strap around his neck holding a device he couldn't quite see in the darkness, and then nodded. He was enjoying the music. But *not* watching everyone else have a good time. His slumped posture screamed this to anyone who glanced in his direction (usually to see whether any more food had come out of the kitchen).

'I see they've got you on clean-up duty,' the man chuckled, slapping Mikey a little too hard on the back. Mikey shrugged.

'Clearly I'm not doing a very good job,' he said, referencing the dirty plates and cutlery around him. The man ignored him and took a seat facing a young woman in a canary yellow, cap-sleeve dress on the dancefloor, who'd been shuffling around arhythmically with her little friends all night. She was a bad, bad dancer. But '*bwoi!*' Mikey heard himself exclaim as they both looked on in awe.

'Bill Lewis,' the man said to Mikey with an outstretched hand, his eyes still on the captivating woman in yellow, whose skirt billowed up around her like a parachute when she moved. Mikey took his hand and shook it back, introducing himself in a similarly distracted manner. The woman, one of several to notice the dashing man, finally locked eyes with Bill, whose hips were jerking so much in his seat he may as well have been dancing with her already. Rising slowly from his chair, as if transfixed, Bill removed the black and silver Kodak Retinette camera and tan holder from around his neck and placed it next to Mikey.

'Have fun with this, little man. If you're gonna watch people all night, you might as well document it.'

Mikey had no idea what Bill was talking about at first; he was still eyeing the crowd, looking at how they moved as a collective, and how each person stood out on their own. His mother was dishing up food in the kitchen again. He could tell by the way she was slapping fritters onto the flimsy foil platter that she had run out of other food options and was worried – unnecessarily – about it. His father was winking at her through the serving hatch from across the dancefloor, oblivious to her stress, and having what looked like the time of his life. The American had, over the course of just two songs, already moved onto someone else: a Indo-Caribbean woman with curly brown hair.

Mikey picked up the camera. It was cold to the touch. Weightier than he'd imagined. Except for that one time he'd gingerly fingered the Brownie camera belonging to his friend William when he was out of sight, he'd never held one before, and he wondered how to do it right, how to capture what he was seeing in reality. He held it up to his face and peered through the viewfinder, unsure as to what the circular ring around the protruding part was, but familiar enough to know which button to press when he wanted to take a picture. He looked over at his parents again – his mother spreading foil over a serving platter with the new batch of steaming fritters; his father still dancing, still watching her – and froze. Whatever it was that kept his father's eyes on his mother, whatever it was that kept her in almost constant servitude, through no one's will but her own, was fascinating to him. It felt like a moment you should be able to reach out and touch. And he wanted to make it so. Mikey tentatively raised the camera to his eye once more, stuck his tongue from the corner of his mouth for maximum precision, and hoped for the best. *Click.*

A bow-legged, light-skinned man stooped low in his navy, wide-legged trousers, caught his eye next. The fabric highlighted the thinness of his legs with every drunken jerk to Mighty Sparrow's 'Royal Jail', the cloth swishing against what looked like two twigs, as others tried their best to salvage their drinks from being knocked over. Mikey found the contrast hilarious. The man looked ecstatic, much to the displeasure of everyone around him. And his ability to keep his own beverage in its plastic cup, no matter how low he dipped, or how fast he moved, and despite spilling everyone else's, was a thing of wonder.

Click.

Though the party was winding down, it was still buzzing outside, as if the place was too ram-packed for the gaggle of smokers and hangers-on round the front of the restaurant. They'd been out there all evening, sending howling laughter and plumes of smoke into the Notting Hill night sky as passers-by looked on, or crossed the street to avoid them. Mikey walked through the cloud of cigarette and weed smoke, letting it filter into his nostrils in the hope of a contact high. No such rush came, but the sight of them was, like the man inside and his parents, almost as satisfying. There were fedora-clad men leaned over giggling women slouched against walls, a familiar white face: Jack Brown, the local drunk who'd never say no to the offer of a little tipple and what he called the 'best party in town'. Leroy Daley, another well-known face in the neighbourhood, mostly because of his access to what Jack also called the 'best weed in town', was out there too, chewing inconspicuously on a frayed toothpick away from the crowd, as if to say: 'If you need me, mi 'ere. But nuh budda come near me fi no passa-passa.' The inaudible public-service announcement seemed to be working. As if protected by an invisible force field, a perfect circle of bodies had gathered just far enough away for him to go virtually unnoticed, but close enough to chime in when their discussion piqued his interest. As a woman rejected the advances of the man who'd been breathing stale beer breath directly into her face with a crisp kiss of her teeth, Leroy took his cue to offer a mocking 'Woi! Better luck next time.' A customer of Leroy's, the man knew better than to react unfavourably, shrugging his shoulders and laughing and waving his hand away to suggest 'she wasn't even that pretty to begin with', though everyone who'd been watching out of the corner of their eyes knew better. Mikey, who was mere metres away from the man, allowed himself a badly timed, quiet snigger as he reached to lift his new toy to capture the moment. No sooner had he done so, the hot sting of a clip around his ear stopped him in his tracks.

'Ah who give yuh dat, pickney?' his father's voice boomed. He was standing behind him now, hand firmly on his right shoulder, squeezing it as a warning about hanging around where he wasn't supposed to be. Mikey attempted to swallow, the bone-dryness of his throat stinging as trace amounts of saliva struggled to travel down it. It didn't matter that he hadn't done anything wrong. The smirk on his face gave it away before he'd had a chance to stifle it: he was having too much fun.

'So, instead of clearin' up an' – an'' – he was stuttering now. Too much beer, evidently – 'an' *helping* yuh mudda' – but you weren't either, Mikey briefly thought about saying – 'yuh just teef the supmn deh, *relax*, look pon people and tek picha?' Mikey ducked his head to dodge a second clip round the ear. His father's eyes bulged.

'Mi nah tek nothing, Daddy. Mi *swear* it.'

His father scoffed, half enjoying his son's scrambling.

'I'll go back in now and help mummy, okay? I was just—'

'Say, champ! You making good use of that camera?'

It was the American soldier again, swaying a little more than he had been earlier, and now with a different woman on his arm – a strong-limbed, brown-skinned beauty who'd been tearing up the dancefloor all night. Mikey's father looked back and forth between them both, unsure as to what to make of the situation.

'The name's Bill Lewis, sir,' the soldier offered, outstretching his hand and bowing a little. Mikey's father, still yet to offer his hand in return, looked him up and down in silence, begrudgingly muttering 'cool, cool' under his breath as he sized him up. Mikey could see that the crispness of the man's uniform, each angle sharper than the next, highlighting his clearly buff physique, had intimidated his father, whose modest belly had ballooned into a protruding, beer-hardened monstrosity over the years. Leaving little room for a reprise of the cussing he had been sure to get before this chance interaction interrupted them, Mikey stepped forward to chime in.

'Mr Lewis let me hold his camera for a while, Daddy ... mi did try fi tell yuh before.' He whispered the last part, just in case. Catching the sass, his father raised his eyebrows, clearly unsatisfied by this vague explanation, and this strange American pretty boy's part in it.

'For a while?' said Bill, whose confusion was just as perplexing to Mikey. Was he in the process of being chucked under the bus? The man had said he could hold it, nuh true?

'But ... well, you said I could ... have fun? Y-you gave it to me and said ... I think ...'

Mikey dared not look up now. He could feel the heat of his father's glare burning a hole into the back of his neck. And that smirk on the GI's face was pissing him right off. What a little snake, he thought, almost forgetting himself and kissing his teeth.

Bill craned his neck to reach Mikey's eye level, his lips wobbling under the pressure of trying to remain serious. He looked at both men once more, took a step back on his right foot and crossed his arms in playful frustration.

'Seems we've got a mystery on our hands, here,' he said, before bursting out laughing. His pecs danced in his top as he did so, much to the delight of the woman who'd now nestled her body into his.

'Don't worry, little man. That was supposed to be a *gift*. It's yours.' Bill patted Mikey on the head once more.

'Sir, you don't have to ... he has enough already,' Mikey's father said.

'And so do I.'

Before he could respond, Bill saluted and thanked Mikey's stupefied father for a 'wild night' and sauntered off into the night with the doting lady in tow. Mikey and his father watched the figures as they moved on ahead down towards Golborne Road, their bodies seemingly twisting and jumping under the soft glow of the moonlight above. Mikey stroked the icy crevices of his new camera once more, the flow of the movement of his fingertips disrupted by the odd scratch or dent from wear and tear. Though they hadn't so much as exchanged a few words, he felt as if he'd just been in the presence of a spirit, a guardian angel of some kind. He raised his camera again, hoping there was enough light on the street to capture their figures. *Click.*

Chapter Five: Gone a Foreign

(Linstead, St Catherine, 2012)

Three months and Frank still wasn't used to the heat. It had never been this close when he was a child. He remembered cool breeze, barely breaking into a sweat even during raucous games, climbing Julie mango trees with ease. Now, it was oppressive. Tiny beads of sweat gathered on his forehead and at the bridge of his nose, no matter how many times he wiped them away. They stung his sun-burned skin as they travelled across the crevices of his face, lines that he was sure hadn't existed when he was back home. 'Home-home.' England.

'Tek time bwoi tek time,' a sarcastic, deep voice boomed. Frank had been daydreaming again, instead of hauling the heavy wheelbarrow across the dusty work yard – the site of someone's soon-to-be home in the sun, about three months from completion. He'd secured the gig after months of bad luck, when Rush, a cousin who'd taken him in, introduced him to the sneering man who was now towering over him.

'Yeah, man, I've got work for you. We'll talk,' the bossman smirked, after a brief discussion on Rush's porch at his insistence a few weeks earlier. Frank didn't like the man's incessant leering then, and he didn't like it now. But he needed to start making money.

'Mi nuh know wah dem do inna h'Inglan, but over here suh? We work. *Hard.* And we don't complain and daydream when there's work to be done. Get back to it.'

No one had spoken to him like that in adulthood. Frank rose from a squat at the edge of the construction site, a position he'd chosen, just far enough away from the other workers to avoid having to talk, but near enough that they couldn't accuse him of being antisocial.

Careful not to let his quizzical gaze turn into a glare, he offered an apology by way of a hard, single nod, then turned to pick up the rusty handles he'd set down five minutes earlier, when the weight of the wheelbarrow and the temperature outside had become too much to bear. *Slave-master mentality,* he thought to himself, knowing there was nothing he could do about it. *Best not call him 'massa'.*

As alienated as Frank felt at work, he was well liked by his colleagues. One or two of them either knew someone or had personally experienced overseas immigration controls themselves; they understood having your world come crashing down. Better yet, whatever their histories, they knew how backbreaking it was to do this job day in, day out.

The wood splinters embedded under calloused skin. The cuts and aching joints. They all told a story of endurance. It connected them in a blood pact of hard labour. It was what they were used to, yes, but it didn't mean they felt satisfied.

To Frank's new manager, a man who, on his own insistence, went solely by 'Boss', even outside of work, this 'British bwoi' as he called him, was an idiot. A pretty boy. Lazy. Wutless.

A pickney, albeit two years his junior. Boss would have heard the rumours about his six children in the UK, about his lack of motivation to work.

'TREE months?!' He remembered how Boss guffawed when Rush told him how long Frank had been out of a job since being deported. Said it so loud that Frank heard it from his bedroom, though he was eavesdropping already, eager to find out the outcome of this third attempt to win Boss over.

It was clear from the off that Boss, with his beer belly and hard hat at all times, despite *his* work being only barking orders, felt threatened by Frank. He wanted an excuse to get rid of him. Frank wouldn't give him one.

He spent the next few hours pushing himself. He sawed wood until the pressure from the handle against his index finger and thumb made them numb. He helped to lay the beginnings of the foundations of the house. He made small talk. He transported load after load of rubbish away from the site whenever Boss got bored and wanted to see Frank sweat even more. He skipped the opportunity for after-work drinks – a few beers by the dusty roadside before home. He preferred to shower, get straight into bed and light up a spliff. Always wondering whether tomorrow, perhaps, he'd be more acclimatised to the heat.

Frank slept. A lot. It was a growing concern in the house, which he shared with his cousin Rush, Rush's pregnant girl-friend, Mandy, and Rush's parents (his aunt and uncle, Trudy and James). It made sense at first, when jet lag was offered as an excuse for the first week, and then another, even if they knew what was really fuelling the lethargy: the sadness. Now, they were all past the point of tiptoeing around. Rush, Mandy and, when they could manage it, Trudy and James, had all tried to confront him about it in their own ways.

Frank would always smile through the interventions. He was 'sweet', he'd maintain. He just needed to get used to everything. In truth, he missed his kids, his job, even missed the blustery weather and how it fucked with his old Volvo. *Truuuu-dy, Jaaaa-mes, Russsssh, Mand-yyyyy*, he'd insist, drawing out each name playfully – he wasn't 'losing' himself. No, he had faith. He was happy. Just look at his face.

The smile wasn't convincing. You could barely see it in the darkness of his bedroom. The curtains were always drawn. But even removed from the dust-laden mist of the rarely aired-out room, it showed. A grin on the verge of breaking, aching to return to its slack state. He'd throw his head back a little too far when people spoke to him, eyes would dart back and forth when they lingered a little longer than he was comfortable with. He didn't bathe. He couldn't. Except sometimes when the kids called.

In his second week, a cousin had given him a SIM card with enough data for video calling. Shame got the better of him, then. He would sometimes brush his teeth – he accepted the intense stare-offs with his own reflection. He was hairier, pickier and dustier than ever. When the self-loathing was intense enough, he'd run a bristle brush over his coils too. Enough to stave off suspicion from his kids through that dodgy 3G internet connection. He'd often wanted to die.

The tricks, as he thought of them, helped. He got a job. Finally. After the fourth ask and the sudden departure of one of his contactors, Bossman begrudgingly let Frank start working. He had to convince other people that he was up to it. Instead of slacking off, he'd work harder than his body could. Family members couldn't then question him beelining to his room after work, burying himself under his covers for the evening. He was a working man now, wasn't he? A suicidal man couldn't do that. Could he?

'I never said anything about nuh *suicide*, Frank,' said Rush – blessed with his nickname in childhood because he couldn't keep still or do anything at less than a frantic pace. Rush had caught a glimpse of despair in his cousin's eyes when he thought no one was watching one too many times to be convinced that everything was okay. He'd seen that look in Frank's eyes, that barely there fog of defeat. The last thing he wanted was to make Frank feel shame. It had been months since Frank last accepted a call from his own children.

Rush slapped Frank's back. 'Listen. Today fi me, tomorrow fi yuh. Your time will come.'

Chapter Six: The Landlord

(Tottenham, 2007)

Delroy had known he'd be successful in business from the moment, aged twelve, he'd oversold his first bag of produce to a customer. A gangly, gap-toothed, confident pickney, he'd been deemed old and sensible enough to help out on his grandmother's fruit stall one scorching Friday afternoon, a duty only his older cousin had been given before she moved to St Elizabeth that summer. It had been over a year since he stopped going to school. Full-time working life felt like an extended punishment for being naughty, except longer and more arduous.

'Yuh tink seh food an' wata spring from the ground like magic?' Delroy's father would ask when he caught him panting from carting heavy wheelbarrows across ploughed soil, or taking extended breaks to drink to waste time. The idea of standing in the barely cool shade, taking instructions and withstanding stinging clips around the ear from his grandmother hadn't seemed much fun to him either. But it trumped working under the watchful yellow eyes of his impatient father on the farm. For one thing, grandma always had a spare stool; his back and feet wouldn't ache as much.

At the market, he could talk as much as he wanted, without remarks like 'yuh mout' set pon spring' from his father and uncle. And there were no beatings. His grandmother was glad for the entertainment.

As long as it served a purpose, his grandmother would say, privately glad for the entertainment. Arthritis had begun to set in, restricting her formerly dexterous fingers. A little chit-chatting wouldn't do any harm – especially if it was bringing in customers. And boy, did Delroy deliver.

'What a pickney cyaan chat,' her customers would often remark, so distracted by his charm that they barely noticed the inflated prices, the tartness of the Otaheite apples he promised were 'sweet like honey', or the occasional force-ripened ackees he sold to wealthy-looking out of towners. It was a lesson in reading people, who, like children's picture books, were laughably easy to study.

The opportunities kept growing after that. Clothes, music, drugs, people – a true ginnal, he could sell them all, swindling everyone from customer to employee, growing his profits – and a dream of flying to live in the UK. Sex work was the perfect business for him. He'd been a small-time dealer in London for the first few years after his arrival. But even with the sadistic edge he'd acquired through cheating others he wasn't cut out for it. Not even money could placate his fear of the reckless violence that sometimes came with that job. But women? Women he could control.

Shirley – a pretty, fiery little white girl he'd met at a dancehall rave – was the first. She looked at him like she believed everything he said. Like she needed to. He told her what she wanted to hear in exchange. Or at least when his actions caused her to question him. It was the other women at first. That quickly became normalised because 'mi cyaan help dat mi a gyalis'. Then it was coaxing her to join him in bed with some of those women. Then hinting at his desire for her to sleep with a friend or two – first for pleasure, then for money, which they initially split between them. Shirley was reluctant at first; even with an admittedly large sexual appetite, she'd had no desire to do it for a living. Delroy, as ever, was convincing. The money would get them both out of their respective situations – and into a place of their own. Everything was a means to an end. Shirley's work helped pay rent on that flat. Eventually, Delroy's provision of girls to his posh landlord and mates added a discount and a little extra on top for him. Everyone was happy. If they weren't, Delroy would show them why they ought be grateful.

Lisa was the seventh woman he forced to see the light. She'd started off as a regular tenant, overwhelmed by the chaotic loneliness of London, eager to do whatever she could to secure a better life. She was smart, and harder to figure out than most, Delroy thought at the time. But he'd get there eventually. And did. When the cleaning company she worked for stopped calling, Delroy knew she'd knock on his door.

'Delroy, you in?' she had bleated, poking her pretty face around the door to his and Shirley's bedroom. Though it had happened years ago, he remembered details; the fear and acceptance in her eyes, the way she'd made her body smaller. After a drunken run-in the night before, they both knew then that she was about to do something she'd never considered. It had made him grow hard. Not hiding his excitement, he remembered gesturing for her to take a seat next to him on the edge of his bed. He stroked her face, stared into her eyes, let out a hot, cigarette-stale sigh and said: 'Baby love, yuh finally come round?'

Who'd have thought she'd stick with him for this long? What began as occasional work turned into Lisa's main profession. She would, sometimes, alongside Shirley, see clients in the flat as Delroy kept watch. When the police raided the adjacent block, putting fear into Delroy and his ever-elusive landlord, the clients were served in hotels. It worked out well, even after Lisa's prudish cousin, Judith, moved in. While her God-fearing, judgemental nature gave Judith the confidence to snub the job, they could all carry on as usual, telling her nothing about what was happening. For Lisa especially, he knew his silence was everything. When his landlord asked him to let him see her in a more private setting – his home – in exchange for a higher than usual fee, he knew what he – and she – would do.

Delroy had met William years before when he was still dealing. William, married, middle-class father of three with a job in the city, would meet him in the litter-infested cul-de-sac (at what he referred to as the 'lower-income end of the street' to Delroy's face).

'Better to keep things discrete that way, moy bredd-ah,' he'd added at the time, unaware of how clumsy his patois sounded tumbling out of his mouth. Though they had their reservations about one another, their relationship grew into something resembling mutual respect. Delroy liked that this rich white man was filth. That, like him, his urge to satisfy his needs could take over. William would get cheap access to any girl he wanted; Delroy would get a discount on rent and a healthy tip on top of the cut he was already making from the girls.

This latest request was a test of that relationship. Though the nature of the appointment hadn't been discussed, he'd heard years of William's dirty stories; William's stated desire to 'really ravage a woman, you know, none of this roleplay stuff. The real deal, man. *Taking* someone. Really *taking* them. Getting carried away,' gave him an inkling. That's why he wanted it to happen in his house. If things got a little rough, he could control the situation. Control the girl. He didn't feel it would be a mistake to indulge him. Delroy had something his landlord desperately wanted. There was always a price for desperation. He'd give him a hard time to negotiate the best fee; he wasn't going to judge the man for being honest about what he wanted. He'd give William full access to Lisa's body, and handle her after.

Judith's dreams of home life in Port Antonio, the birthplace of her parents, and theirs before them, had not stopped in the months since her arrival in London. Each morning, she'd wake up with a start, her worlds melding into a hazy nightmare that kept the comforts of home just out of reach. Sometimes, when reality felt particularly cruel, she'd squeeze her eyes tightly shut and try to fall back into her dream state, longing for its false comforts. She wanted more than anything to open her eyes and see the blurred wooden-blade arms from the ceiling fan in her bedroom whirring above her once more, like she had for the past twenty years of her life. She pined for the lush, rolling hills that once framed the view from her old bedroom window. Even for the buzzing mosquitos eager for a taste of her blood or the tiny lizards that occasionally scaled the cool white walls that encased her octagonal-shaped bedroom.

Most of all, she missed the quiet stirring from her mother's room down the hall of their bungalow. The reminder that, in spite of her declining health, she was still here. Still a busy-body. Still in reach. What she got instead were discoloured brown and orange bricks from the drab British building opposite, noise pollution from the busy road outside and a deep sense of bewilderment. No one had warned her, in the months before she made the trip to London, how much she'd miss that view. How much she'd miss feeling like she was exactly where she was supposed to be.

Back home, she'd usually be up well before the sun's beams turned the taupe-blue sky golden. Her body clock had been trained to wake her just before the cocks from the local farm had begun their morning crows, when everything felt still and cool, save for the light breeze that disturbed banana, bread-fruit and palm leaves nearby, making them whisper. She'd start her day boiling mint or fevergrass tea from the yard, fixing breakfast – usually some variation of hard food, fried bammy and ackee or cornmeal porridge – her favourite. By the time it was cooling on the stove, she'd make a short walk to the store on the roadside to pick up a copy of the *Gleaner*, flashing a smile at sweet-faced Garnet, the coy shop owner who'd loved her off since they were teenagers, and honoured that bond through discounts and longing glances. She'd have married and had kids with him in another life. She was sure of it – had her father not fallen ill all those years ago, or her capacity to let herself fall in love not been consumed by a need to give it all to her family instead.

Though he'd held on for some time, dropping in each day to see her and slinking away when she gradually cut their interactions short, then off completely – save for buying the daily paper – Garnet eventually found a new love: a mindless, mawga girl twenty years her junior who, when she was there, seemed far more interested in her mobile phone than interacting with her man or any other customers. On the front porch of her family home, where she'd steal fifteen minutes to herself each day before tending to her mother, Judith would allow herself to appreciate those morning nods and his small talk, moments that meant more to her than he'd ever know. She was confident he felt the same way.

With mother fed, bathed and medicated, Judith would make her way down the steep hill that snaked down from the house and down to the main road that led to town. Whether enduring long queues for ATMs sandwiched between colonial, pillared buildings, or jostling for the good fruit at the market, she'd found comfort in the routine of daily life. Sure, prickles of loneliness would momentarily disturb her if she let her mind wander. But there was no shortage of errands to keep those base desires at bay. There were church sisters to drop in on, calls to make to her brother and sister with updates on their mother's health, trips to the pharmacy and, when the day was over, shifts at the sprawling Sunshine Lagoon – a grand old resort, crumbling at the foundations – where she worked as a receptionist. The only luxuries she allowed herself really were biannual visits to the chaotic city to see her nieces and nephews and odd afternoon visits to Cee Lee's Jerk Kitchen in Boston Bay for fatty, flavourful portions of jerk pork and tangy, green jerk sauce, which she ate by the roadside, eyes closed, spirit ascended.

Judith hadn't arrived at her decision to leave easily. In fact, she hadn't arrived at it at all. Were it not for the encouragement of her mother, whose face cracked with deepening pity the more frail she became, Judith would never have entertained the prospect of studying abroad, let alone pursuing the career she'd always dreamed of. She was doing it in everything but name already, wasn't she? As old age rendered her mother less mobile, less lucid, no qualified nurse Judith encountered could touch her when it came to attention to detail. To them, her mother was a patient. To Judith, she was everything.

'Judith,' her mother would say with that knowing, worried gaze. A gaze that, after years of caring for her, told Judith it was best not to respond.

'Juuuuditttt . . .' she'd add, lowering her gaze.

'Yes, mummy,' Judith would respond, trying her best to fixate on whatever task – cooking, bathing, cleaning – was at hand.

'When yuh ah guh leff me an' find a man?'

Which man it was didn't matter. It was a comment that represented an idea. Her way of telling her daughter to live her life. Judith could ignore those efforts most days. Whether she came right out with it, coyly dropped information about some church sister's grandson, or – when the passage of time eluded her senile mind – Garnet, the comments washed over Judith like water on wax. But it became harder when the focus on her love life gave way to the one dream of becoming a nurse that she'd kept alive in the back of her mind.

Judith had spent the majority of her life taking on responsibility for everyone in her family with the sense of duty
that burdens eldest daughters. She wielded the bush broom
on the yard outside like an expert, combing over the dirt
with such effort that it almost gave off a sheen. She took to
hand-washing as if it were sport, producing the customary
scrupsie-scrupsie sound her little sister and brother never
quite managed to pick up from their mother. What to her
younger siblings were chores they grudgingly performed,
leaving her to fix their half-hearted efforts lest their parents
see, was to her an inherited sense of pride in keeping an im-
maculate home and her family well cared for, no matter what.

When her brother and sister went to university and
eventually married off, leaving the country for the big city –
Kingston – with their new families, Judith stayed behind,
living and working just a few short minutes away in case her
parents needed her. When their father, a quietly commanding
retired police officer, was diagnosed with stomach cancer that
same year, she turned down a nursing scholarship and took
on home-caring responsibilities instead. When it worsened
six months later, violently ripping him and his spirit from
the family, she moved back in, hoping to distract her dazed
mother from the hole her father's departure had created.
She'd remained there throughout her thirties, forties and now
fifties. But it wasn't sustainable these days. Not financially.
She'd worked service and hospitality jobs all her life, cutting
her teeth at hotels around town as a maid and, eventually,
receptionist. She took work as seriously as her duties at home,
approaching her shifts at the Sunshine Lagoon with as much
attention to detail as she eventually applied to caring for her

mother, with no extra pay to show for it – particularly during the quiet seasons.

Judith would have gone on pretending that deferred dream was a silly fantasy if she'd had any choice in the matter. It was easier to accept things as they were. Until it wasn't.

'Judith . . .' her mother started again between mouthfuls of chocho, saltfish and green banana one sweltering afternoon. Her tone was devoid of its usual playfulness. There was fatigue behind it. She wiped her wet brow and then the corners of her lips with a paper towel and folded it dutifully, setting her hands on the table before her as if chairing a meeting. Judith's heart sank.

'Yes, mummy?' she replied. Her mother's eyes, wide and watering, were wavering. Her bottom lip was quivering. She took her soft, frail hand in hers.

'Live. Your. Life.' She punctuated each word with a gentle squeeze. Judith sighed and opened her mouth to respond, all the words in the world lodged in her mind. She squeezed her mother's hand back and closed her eyes, hoping they'd hold back welling tears that she was sure were about to burst forth.

'Mi nuh care wah yuh haffi do. Guh ah foreign. Guh find a man. But don't live your life for me. Yuh know mi 'av two other pickney?'

Judith laughed and shook her head, feeling a weight she didn't know was there lift from her body.

'I know how bad it bun yuh when you turned down that scholarship all those years ago, Judith, because it hurt me too.'

Judith opened her mouth to speak as her mother pressed a finger against it, then began rifling through the dog-eared black leather notebook she kept in the side bag on her wheelchair. She leafed through with urgency, muttering to herself as she searched for whatever it was that she was on the hunt for.

'Ah. Yes,' she added, stabbing at a row of neatly scrawled digits in the middle of a cluttered page.

'Ah dat your cousin Lisa number. Remember?'

Judith's eyes widened. Lisa's name was more often brought up in whispers in those days. If it wasn't conjecture about her sexuality, it was gossip about how well Lisa's mother appeared to be living. The new car she'd bought herself. The new clothes. How 'Lisa mussa rich now'. She hadn't spoken to her cousin for a good couple of years, but they had been close once upon a time. Before the rumours. Why was her mother bringing her up? Had she forgotten that too? Judith looked at her mother with desperation, then fixed her face as she looked up from her notebook and continued.

'Mi call 'ar last week. She say she have a *nice* flat inna di city, ennuh? Near ... mi think she say Tottenham Court Road? Sista Brown told me that's a very nice part of town. Very nice.' Judith's mother was nodding now. She had never been to the UK, nor had she ever had any desire to go. But she had been increasingly seduced by the idea of her daughter making the trip, pushing her to talk to anyone who had made the long journey and found their lives miraculously awash with prosperity. Had Judith not made the call to her cousin and swiftly found that going back to school wasn't the pipe dream she initially thought but a sensible prospect, she'd probably still be with her mother, glad to give her more years of her life. Instead, she felt stuck in a rat race, sending more money than she'd ever made abroad – yet avoiding calls that made her feel pressured into whitewashing her situation, just like she realised Lisa had had to. Later that night, when her sister's face flashed across her screen, she readied herself for the charade once again, wondering what it would take – between the hostile newspaper headlines about immigrants, violent outbursts from Delroy, daily racism, and Lisa's life-style – for her to give up entirely.

Chapter Seven: The March

(Central London, 1963)

Mikey had enjoyed snaking his way in and out of the crowds, through side streets, cul-de-sacs and back again. When there was a protest on, something in the air changed. Almost like the feeling he had at his first bacchanal in London, the year after Mr Cochrane died. There was so much that could happen – and he wanted to see it all, even on the periphery of the excitement. What did the chatter, the sounds of 'ban the bomb, ban the bomb', and the music sound like to the people wrapped up warm in their houses? No desire to join the ranks on the streets of London, to march to the tune of 'The H-bomb's Thunder'. Only the wherewithal to poke their heads out of their windows or smoke their cigarettes on their front steps. Didn't they know how ... *exciting* all this was?

The eighteen-year-old smiled meekly at a head-scarved woman in a heavy coat, puff-puff-puffing away while the sounds of the CND rally echoed in the near distance. She raised her tattooed eyebrow in response and continued to blow smoke out of her nose. The woman had clearly come out to get a glimpse of the protesters but she'd dare not cross the street and turn the bend to meet the crowds face to face. Even so, as the stragglers filtered into the side roads, she got what she wanted. Mikey, now leaning against a lamp-post on the opposite side of the road, had spotted his next shot. Raising his camera slowly to his face, he caught it: two demonstrators with NUCLEAR DISARMAMENT placards held in their hands, skipping after one another, while a miserable-looking head-scarfed woman stared on after them in the background.

'Fucking hippy nutters!' she shouted after spotting Mikey, who chose the moment to follow the couple back to the march, convinced he'd got the shot to put him on the map.

As the Strand became Trafalgar Square, the couple Mikey was following disappeared. Though he recognised few faces in the crowd, he was glad to rejoin the throng, chanting the odd word to slogans he'd heard earlier in the day. The call for an end to the use of nuclear weapons felt like release. So did any cause deemed 'for the people'. He embraced everything and rejected it; knew it was worth knowing more about, while refusing to delve deeper. Everything he needed to know, he would say to awestruck women who fell into his arms at events like these, was in their eyes. His Retinette could capture that just fine. He believed in banning the bomb, wanted peace for all and hated racism with all his heart. Getting the chance to drink, meet people and pick up a girl wasn't a bad outcome for fighting those evils.

Mikey craned his neck forwards to make direct eye contact with Lilian, the white girl he'd been talking with a couple of hours ago. She had been doing the same and made no secret of her eagerness to talk to him again, waving him over with the enthusiasm of an old sweetheart. Mikey was drawn to her in a way that made him feel uncomfortable. She was a pretty girl, like other pretty girls, but it was who she was that made her more attractive. He could tell from her accent and nice clothes that she was wealthy. At least some class or other above his. The milky whiteness of her skin, though he hated himself for fixating on it, added to the allure.

He was captivated, scared. Was this how it started? The relationships with white girls that garnered funny looks from the locals in his area? He didn't know whether he wanted to find out.

'You disappeared! I thought I'd never see you again,' said Lilian, who he'd found out earlier was seventeen, a year younger than him. She grabbed his arm as she said it, pulling him closer than they probably should be in public.

Mikey's accent disappeared when he talked to her. The way it evaporated in school when his teacher tried to make him feel stupid: 'You're in England now, you should at least know the language.'

There was no trace of a 'mi' anywhere. 'H's were emphasised to the point of silliness, vowels twisted into something resembling plumminess, but not quite. It was an impression of how he thought someone like Lilian would want him to sound, more than anything else.

'How did you find me?' he chuckled, winking at Lilian as he tipped his grey pork-pie hat forward.

'Didn't take much looking in this crowd!' she added, pleased with herself.

Mikey laughed, unsure of how to respond. So he didn't, leaving the pair to walk in uncomfortable silence for thirty seconds or so. Irritating as those comments were to him, he liked having the edge over her. Making her stew in her igno-rance for as long as he liked.

'I'm hungry,' said Lilian, attempting to salvage the conversation.

'Yuh wan' – I mean, do you want us to look for something to eat? I know a couple of places.'

Lilian looked into Mikey's eyes with an expression that was full of expectation. It scared him as much as it made his heart flutter.

'Something in my eye?' he said, trying to solidify his melt-ing face.

Lilian shook her head and smiled. 'I would like that very much, Mikey.'

The pair broke off from the crowd with ease, slipping down a side street and onto a bus as if playing a game of hide and seek. They'd move from rant to rant, bashing the idiocy of war and racism in one moment, and embracing the allure of revolution in the next. Mikey's pride was too big to admit how out of depth he felt about these talks. The thrill of ral-lying with the righteous had become a favourite way to spend time. Parsing the issues being battled against was a different story. When it came down to it, he felt like a poser.

'I just *love* everything about Cuba,' said Lilian in between mouthfuls of sponge cake. They'd found a poky yet cosy café with a bottle-green Vitrolite exterior in west London that Mikey often used as a pit stop on his trips around the area – looking for inspiration, seeking ways to make money or just setting out to meet someone new. He was finding it hard to listen to Lilian. He didn't want to talk about Castro, or Batista, or whatever. It was idealistic and beyond him. Strange too that this little white girl was positioning herself to lead the charge 'for the people', as she kept on repeating. *He* was used to being the overbearing, righteous one in the room. Who did Lilian, with her sordid fascination with movements that didn't affect her, think she was?

Mikey looked up at Lilian, who was still, as she always seemed to be, in the middle of an impassioned speech.

'I mean, just *think*, Mikey. Think what sort of change you and I could bring!'

Mikey scoffed.

'And what would your parents think?'

Lilian ignored him and began to toy with the last morsel of the cake she'd been so enjoying. Mikey felt bad for upsetting her, but more so because of the all-consuming silence that had since taken over the room, save for the clanging of crockery in the kitchen, and the odd slurp from the one other customer in the room opposite them. Giving up the battle with the small piece of sponge she'd been moving around the plate before her, Lilian popped it into her mouth indignantly.

'All the evils of the world are counting on us, Mikey, to remain divided. The Black man from the white man. Women from men. The pacifists from the militarists. And here we are, saying, Fuck you, man. Fuck you! *I'll* talk to anyone I want. Lie down with *anyone* I want, you know?'

Mikey furrowed his brows.

'Lie down?'

Lilian smirked and took a sip of her coffee before meeting his eye.

'Lie down ... stand up ... bend over for ...'

The pair broke out into laughter.

'Are we talking about what I think we're talking about?'

Lilian ran her fingers through her mousy brown hair, interlocked her hands under her chin and nodded. Though Mikey was drawn to her, he knew now wasn't the time. He wanted to take more photos, to lose himself in another crowd. He wanted to lose Lilian. Not for ever. But for now, at least. Their flirting, though fun, had run its course about an hour and a half ago. And there was no way he was going to risk trying to sneak some white girl to his parents' flat in the middle of the day. The news would be out before he even put the key in the lock.

'Lilian, I can't.'

Her face sank. Mikey explained himself further, that as much as he enjoyed her company tonight wasn't the time. She seemed incensed. Except this was a quiet, burning irritation that didn't come out in outbursts or speech. She didn't need those tactics for what she was communicating, her dagger-like eyes and monosyllabic responses did the work. Even when he wrote down the number for the restaurant on his napkin and specified when to call. Even when she did the same, and wrote down her full name, number and address. Pure fire and rage. They'd revisit this soon enough.

Mikey picked up his hat and secured it over his light-brown afro as Lilian stared after him. He thought it strange that someone he'd met only hours ago had grown so attached to him, but it flattered him no less. Perhaps he was turning into a ladies' man after all. Could it be that he, and not this woman, was the prize? As the pair left the café, Mikey took Lilian's hand in his and kissed it gently. As she melted, she smiled once more, shaking her head at what she perceived as teasing.

'It was nice to meet you, Mikey.'

Mikey tipped his hat and began to walk backwards away from her.

'You too. See you soon.'

When Mikey got in that evening, his parents had already closed the shop for the day. It was a detail in their rigid routine that told the young man, before he even turned a key in his front door, that one of them was probably in the middle of fixing dinner, if they hadn't finished already. Exhausted and irritable as they always were at this time, they'd probably be in the mood for asking probing questions. Where had he been? Who had he been with? And did he really think wandering around with a camera was going to earn him the living he was already failing to make? It was always the same. Mikey still wondered why it was that they were so adamant about him 'making it' in a country they talked incessantly about leaving.

As he walked into the living room, where his mother was setting the table, his 'Hello, Mummy, hello, Daddy' was greeted with a silence that he'd come to expect. Until the food had been plated and the cutlery placed just so, that would be all he got. This time, though, as he began to wolf down the stew peas his father had prepared, it felt like it was more than mild generational confusion that had raised a drawbridge between himself and his parents. He suspected they thought he had done something wrong. Mikey looked up at his father for a brief second for reassurance as the vapour from the food and the light behind him briefly conjured up an illusion of steam rocketing from the top of his head. Mikey looked to the right, where his mother sat opposite. There were no comically dramatic fumes shooting from her skull, but her nostrils were flared, a sure sign as any that she was vex. Sensing an opportunity to avoid the round of questioning that was surely coming his way, Mikey began to spoon more food in his mouth than he could possibly swallow in one go as brown-red stew dripped down the corners of his mouth. It took just one chups from his father for him to realise his diversion tactic had failed. Minutes later, through which the dinner had continued in stony silence, four words from his mother revealed a whole lot more. They didn't have to ask where he'd been. They already knew. 'How was the march?' she asked.

'Why?'

Mikey had his first argument with his parents that evening. To be precise, the first in which he argued, really argued, back. Though he was typically unbothered by the scolding he'd come to expect throughout childhood, he didn't understand their anger this time around. And he responded in kind, confused and upset as to why he was being punished, the weight of the world heavy on his frustrated, teenage shoulders.

'Mi nah business bwoi. You are still *my* pickney, mi nah know who say becah yuh a big man now yuh cyaan treat me and yuh mother with respect. Marching around town with the hippy dem like yuh some likkle white pickney. Like the police won't come lick off your headtop just for being there. Damn eediat,' his father spat in response. 'Chat bout "why?" Mi have a mind fi box yuh right now just for that,' he muttered under his breath, unable to stop himself as his wife nodded along in agreement.

Mikey caught on. It had nothing to do with the demonstration. It was the people and why, of all causes, he had chosen to take up one so far removed from the community.

'I don't remember you marching for Jamaica's independence last year,' his mother said, her voice sounding more desperate with anger. Mikey didn't remember any west London march leading to Jamaica gaining its independence, nor, save for the celebration they had at the restaurant, his parents taking part in one. He knew better than to say so.

'Where were your likkle white friends dem when we were fighting for our freedom?' his mother added.

Mikey wanted to talk about how little attention even they paid to it until it had come to pass. There was no 'fighting' for Jamaica or anything when it came to his parents. There was only reminiscing about it, going to work, coming home and doing it all over again. Nothing was challenged, no roots set down, no plans put in place, no matter how often they talked about 'going back home'. They were treading water while he thrashed his way towards an escape, even if there was a chance of him being mistaken for a threat while he did so.

'While you're celebrating the freedom of your country, you're still here, working yourselves to death for the nation that captured it in the first place. You like independence? Try exercising it for once by having an original thought,' he said in the same not-quite-English accent he'd affected in front of Lilian from the march, gearing himself for the blow that was coming.

Chapter Eight: The Passport

(Linstead, 2013)

People referred to the modest, detached yellow bungalow with aloe vera running around the perimeters and its separate, slightly pokier guest house, as 'Trudy and dems''. Though in reality, it was Rush who ran the Linstead household. The ageing matriarch and patriarch were rarely seen by visitors these days. Alzheimer's had taken hold in James. Arthritis had consumed Trudy's gnarled body. Fond neighbourhood memories of their bickering with each other in the garden, sharing out barrels packed with goods from foreign, and sauntering through the market, waving and hollering at every other passer-by, were fading with the older generation who knew them best. Though neither had the warmest of dispositions, they drew in the wayward like high grass to fireflies, offering them practical comforts in place of emotional warmth.

Trudy, whose flowery frocks and bonnets didn't quite match the sternness of her delivery, nor the respect she commanded just by her way of being: selfless, direct and fair – was the more feared of the two. When the kids from next door would skin their teeth and tentatively ask if they could climb her trees with Rush, it often took as little as a shift in her eyes for them to get lost. It was James, the silent shinehead, who gave them a sign to come back later, when her head was turned. It was a dynamic that worked. And when the prying eyes of the neighbours, or their son, Rush, were occupied, the moments they shared in private were tender. If ever Trudy, even in her old age, wondered whether her husband still loved her, she just had to look at him in the quiet moments, when his eyes would warmly scan over her entire body until they met her own gaze. If James ever did, it took little more than a bashful smile and a squeeze of a hand, the same reaction she always had when she had private moments to enjoy his affections. Even with the gulf that Alzheimer's had put between them, when James found moments of lucidness, it was her almond eyes he'd gaze into, her hands he'd refuse to stop caressing.

Rush had been in charge for the past five years, right after his parents took ill and his long-time girlfriend, Mandy, moved in. Living up to his nickname, he took to managing the house like a dutiful housekeeper-cum-care worker. No task was left undone, no issue neglected. With his quiet wit and a tone that could thaw even the frostiest of temperaments, he'd transform run-of-the-mill expressions into poetry with a turn of phrase and a long, hard stare. People trusted him. They respected him, too. He was not the go-to for neighbour-hood issues likes his parents – that was now left to the gossip merchants. He did, however, take after Trudy and James in one significant way: he was who people turned to when they had nowhere else to go, when they knew they needed the ear of someone who wouldn't say a word about their secrets . . . because he had no interest in using them to hurt anyone.

Rush saw everything. They knew he might as well have been blind; he saw without actually seeing. He saw when the Perrys – a proud, respectable family who'd fallen on hard times some years after their patriarch, Derek, was let go from his job at the plant up in Ewarton – began their secret nightly ritual of wading through food waste outside shops and people's homes. And, when things became desperate, in and around the mango trees in Trudy and dems' own garden, globules of sticky juice from their fingers drip-drip-dripping on the sharp grass below as they snuck their way past what they assumed was the sleeping household. Rush, who was often up at strange hours of the morning – it was the only time he had entirely to himself – never told anyone. What were four Julies in the scheme of things?

When he took over early-morning gardening duties from his father James, it was the same story. He saw Mr Grant sneak back from Naomi Ellis's house to his own, heard them giggling as they snuck kisses at the back door when they thought it was safe. He said nothing. These days, he could also see that ever since he'd arrived on that charter flight from England, his cousin Frank was struggling, in recent weeks more than he ever had.

What began on his cousin's arrival worsened each time Frank made a last-ditch attempt to appeal his case. He'd talk about chats he'd had with charity workers, immigration experts, even journalists, who all at various points had told him they could help – until later, beaten by bureaucracy, they revealed they couldn't. What usually followed was a creeping sense of defeat, a force that took over his body from the larynx down, pushing him into dark, lonely silence that, cruelly, only the small hope of being able to leave could lift. Receiving his British passport – with the hope of using it to strengthen his case – was one such source of hope. He'd been told through a friend of Rush's who had helped to connect Frank to a deportation support charity, that his passport was due to arrive at the British High Commission within a matter of weeks. When those weeks passed, and Frank took *that* call, it seemed Frank's hopes of escaping his situation had been dashed yet again.

Rush, who was cutting back the overgrown fever grass bush with a lass at the time, heard Frank take the call with Leroy, the man who ran the service that had been supporting him. In the quiet of the early morning, it was easy for Rush to hear the other end of the conversation if he remained still enough, making out the odd word through the muffled responses as he edged nearer to the veranda where Frank was.

'Weh yuh mean, *them nuh find it?*' Frank said, turning his back as if to give himself a sense of privacy in a place that had ears all over.

'Them claim them send it already,' Rush made out from the voice on the other end of the line, from his spot below the veranda. He'd dropped his machete for a rake now, to maintain the illusion of minding his business, if only to help out later on.

'Wah di ras? *How?*' Frank whispered, briefly catching Rush's eye as he searched his surroundings for some semblance of an explanation as to what was happening to him. 'If dem send it already then why are we having this conversation? Mi nah receive nuttin. The Hembassy nuh have it. Weh it deh? Limbo?' to which a sympathetic voice crooned what – judging by the dejected tone – could only be apologies down the phone. Rush made out a few more words as he got closer.

'... I know. I'm sorry. I will keep ... call on Thursday with ... Home Office.'

This was serious, then. If there was one valuable lesson he had come to learn since Frank crash-landed back into their lives, it was that the words 'sorry' and 'Home Office' were not a hopeful combination. As Frank wrapped up the phone call, his head so deep in his palms that it was hard to tell whether it was sweat or tears rolling down his cheeks, Rush resumed chopping away at the stiff grass, conveying nothing. Aside from reconnecting with his homeland, Frank had lost virtually everything since coming back. Rush wanted to give him the space to hold onto some semblance of his pride, and hung back, collecting stray leaves into a heap.

Later, over bush tea and a spliff that Rush, just over a year into living with Frank, still had to remind him that he didn't smoke, Frank explained why he didn't speak or make eye contact with anyone for a good five minutes afterwards. Why he had broken out of his stupor to whisper a defeated 'shit' under his breath as he leaned his body weight on the yellow, crumbling, wooden railing surrounding the veranda. At the time, he had ignored the polite nudging from Rush, asking him not to lean 'pon the rail suh' when there were plenty of seats – bar Trudy and James's coveted wicker armchairs – for him to take.

His caseworker, Leroy, had explained that his passport, essential to appeal his case, had not in fact been sent to the British High Commission by the Home Office as they had claimed. It wasn't clear where it was. He was rocking so hard on the railing as he relived the bad news that Rush thought one of the planks of wood would snap clean off, giving him one more job to take care of. As Rush was about to scold him, Frank suddenly shot down the shallow veranda steps and began pacing around the aloe-vera- and fever-grass-laden yard. Rush knew he'd need to be more supportive going forward, preparing Frank for the possibility that he might never return to the UK. Day by day, it seemed a more likely outcome than the dream of returning to the country that never wanted him, where neighbours whispered about him being a criminal.

It had been hard for Rush and the rest of the family to watch. They had missed Frank and enjoyed seeing him become more comfortable in the surroundings he once called home all those years ago. The simultaneous descent into darkness was a problem. Despite his consistency at work, his unflinching ability to disappear into hard labour for hours on end – no matter how much he was hurting inside and out – his moods and absenteeism grated on Boss. Even Charmaine, 'the Frank whisperer' of his children, seemed defeated by his calls: monotone updates that nothing had changed and probably never would. There was no use in her worrying about him now. Rush had to step in.

Chapter Nine: The Plantation

(St Catherine, 2013)

The rumours about the 'great house' at the far edge of town, a blindingly white, three-storey estate with more rooms than it had use for, had been circulating for decades. It was haunted, it was cursed, doomed to an eternity of darkness, so plagued was its history with death and exploitation. Hundreds of years after its acquisition by the Jamaican state, local unease was still palpable. Its grandeur was the manifestation of tortured lives made into money. You couldn't drive past that place without part of you wincing, feeling it in your body, changing the pitch of your voice.

The plantation was usually occupied by giddy tourists in high-vis jackets, learning about the age-old art of rum production. The macabre history only alluded to in a general way by the tour guides; proof of torture and routine viciousness had been removed. Yet the faceless duppies responsible for the estate's centuries-long success could be felt: in the gusts of wind that made stray foliage dance; in the heavy security gates, barbed wire, guards and dogs that surrounded the property. The logo for the Happy Rum empire – a splash of imperial red lettering superimposed over a black backdrop – was intended to convey authenticity. In a certain light, it did – by evoking splattered blood. 'Jamaica's Heart' read the tagline, a seemingly warm phrase far more revealing than the far-off advertising firm who proposed it had intended. Along with the gimmicky nineteenth-century cart parked up in front of the signage, it made for chilling viewing for more observant visitors, as though the rictus grin of a corpse had emerged beneath the welcoming smiles of their host. Yet the location was below one of the highest and most beautiful points in town. A hilltop a half-mile away that provided breathtaking views. Here was the history of this place, of the nation. Beautiful from a bird's-eye view, unsettling once you took a second to focus. If you chose to notice it, the beige to light brown hue of the people who still largely held the majority of the country's wealth, the huge profits of European-owned estates peppered around the island, demonstrated that the more things seemed to have changed, the more they stayed the same.

These were Rush's thoughts when he took his daily stroll to the hilltop. Mandy, at eight months pregnant, no longer enjoyed the half-hour drive and hour-long walk. It had taken a while for Rush to realise how tiresome she now found it. A competitive sprinter in her teens, she had always been fitter than him, pushing him to go hiking or fishing or jogging with her when they had a chance. Not any more.

'Rush, unless you're going to help me carry this pickney –' she gestured to her swollen stomach, encased in a red linen sundress that made her skin sing '– up that steep, steep, hill, I'm staying right here. Chat bout, "let's go for a hike",' she said, kissing her teeth, forcing Rush to stifle a guffaw at her indignation. He knew it was a silly thing to suggest the moment the words fell out of his mouth. What was he thinking? Would you and our ten-pound baby like to lug yourselves up the steepest hill for miles, so we can look down and bad-mouth that plantation, then turn to the left a little and admire sugar-cane fields likely belonging to the same grounds?

'Okay, point taken. Yuh need anything from down the road? Can pass tru the market on the way back?'

Mandy smiled at Rush's less than sly attempt to appease her and shook her head.

'Just call me when yuh coming back so mi can heat up the soup in time. I might lie down for a little while.'

'As usual,' Rush retorted with a smirk, making his way to Frank's door. Mandy lobbed a pillow at his head.

Rush rarely spent time with Frank outside the house. He was a get-up-and-go sort of person, up from what o'clock to the late hours every day, keeping himself busy. Though he wished they'd grown closer, Rush saw their ordinary routines were incompatible. With Mandy's absence leaving him bereft, perhaps he could coax Frank to leave the barricade of his room and join him on his walk from time to time – if he approached the situation gently.

'Yuh wan what?' Frank snapped groggily from behind the closed door.

'*Walk*,' Rush replied a little louder.

'Yuh wan fi ... walk? Where? Why?'

Rush opened the door a crack and poked his head around it awkwardly, causing his cousin to recoil slightly.

'Just to get out. There's a nice hilltop over there, suh.'

Rush could sense Frank's embarrassment. It had been a

few weeks since anyone had tried to enter that room, and it stank. Soiled clothes strewn all over the place, empty snack packets on the floor, a cluster of ants feasting on something sticky in the corner. He wanted to cuss Frank out. He knew he couldn't, though, if he wanted to be successful.

'It's about a half-hour drive, and then an hour and a half walk,' Rush added under his breath, trying not to inhale through his nose.

'You wan drive fi walk up a hill?'

'Not just any hill,' said Rush, amused at his cousin's city-dweller ways. Though Frank was as fit as Rush, and had been athletic as a child, he could see his cousin struggling to grasp the idea.

'It magical?' Frank said sarcastically.

'Yeah, man,' Rush said back just as dryly. 'Let's go. Stop asking questions, put some clothes on nuh, man.'

Frank nodded dutifully and grabbed the nearest T-shirt he could find. He moved with pace, as if waiting a second longer would glue him to the spot.

From the moment the sun rose until it set at dusk it beat down on the Happy Rum estate. Its sugar-cane fields offered no hiding place from the glare, and little else, in fact, other than the views of the great house and row after row of horticultural tedium. Just heat, greenery, space and, eventually, fermentation. Most visitors these days came voluntarily for just that. Plantation life stripped of atrocities and shrouded in rustic luxury. As the groups of tourists arrived, they would ooh and aah at a world that once driven thousands to their deaths, excited to drink in that history straight from the source.

'And if you turn this way, you'll see the warehouse where we *age* the rum. We'll be visiting this spot in a little while,' an older white Jamaican man in a salmon linen shirt bellowed to the distracted group behind him, camera phones and digital cameras in front of their faces, as if something unexpected were about to happen. It never did. That was part of the charm.

Rush and Frank had been observing from the car in front of the entrance for ten minutes. 'People watching', Frank kept calling it. They'd exchange glances each time they found something funny, like this tour guide, needlessly raising his voice at small groups of people who could hear him if he whispered. But they were getting looks now. A guard for the estate, a slim and stern-faced Black man that Rush had passed on his drive there countless times, was attempting to edge his way towards the vehicle undetected. He'd seen the pair laughing and carrying on, and seemed to have grown tired of standing still, or brandishing his baton around. Whatever he wanted to do next, it wouldn't be good for either of the cousins.

'What him want?' said Frank, nervously slinking down into his seat as the man continued to advance, but trying to maintain an air of bravado in case he decided to test them.

'Whole heap'a trouble,' Rush replied, fiddling with the handbrake. 'Or some entertainment. Either way, we're not staying to find out.'

He was right. Within ten seconds of gearing themselves up to drive to another spot out of view, the guard's stride had picked up, his baton now swinging round and round with more speed as he spat at the ground beneath him.

'Eh bwoi!' the guard shouted, demanding, as they began to

leave, they answer to him. This was the problem with these guards, Rush thought to himself. Low pay and monotonous, back-aching work. No one to take it out on but the innocent.

'No sah, I couldn't stand in that heat all day,' Rush added, ignoring the guard's attempts to get their attention as the car backed away. In the midst of being troubled by some jobsworth, Rush was sympathetic. *Amazing*, Frank thought to himself. Though he'd never admit it out loud, it was astonishment that was as riddled with admiration as irritation. His do-gooder cousin was a virtuous blessing, and a pain in the arse.

'Chat bout, "Weh yuh ah do?"' Frank said, mocking the man's attempts to intimidate them as they drove to safety, daring Rush to join in with the badmouthing. 'Eh bwoi, eh bwoi,' he added, kissing his teeth and slapping his thigh as if he were amused. Inside, though, he was seething.

Rush, who'd been fatigued by the situation as soon as he'd spotted the guard, turned his attention to the narrow path leading away from the estate and towards the hill. *There were always going to be badmind people, the ones that test you and hope to God you'll give them the reaction they crave,* he thought as the uneven ground beneath them rocked their bodies back and forth. He let out an exaggerated 'woi' and smiled at his wound-up cousin as they pulled up to park.

Rush knew Frank was finding it hard to keep his head down. To mind his business. Especially when Boss, sensing his power over the 'English bwoi', as he called him, would wind him up on purpose. What he needed was stillness, honesty, love.

Not one drop of sweat had soiled Rush's bottle-green

shorts and white vest by the time they made it to the peak. Although Frank was becoming more and more used to the all-over burn that came with toiling in the sun at work, his body was still adjusting. He hadn't taken a single walk since he'd been here. Dripping with salty sweat, he watched as his cousin scaled the hill as if levitating with each step, the twigs and dust beneath his feet carrying him up, up, up.

'You all right back there?' said Rush, from four metres ahead.

'Yeah . . . yeah,' Frank shouted back, his best impression of a young man who loved to hike, and was only taking his time because he wanted to lap up every second.

When they reached the clearing ahead, an oddly manicured expanse, he understood why they were there. It was beautiful.

'Yuh see the magic yet?' Rush asked excitedly, his eyes brighter than usual.

'Yeah man, it's done wonders for your miserable arse,' Frank replied jokingly, still catching his breath.

'*Me? Miserable?*' His voice rose higher when he was surprised, or mildly outraged. In this case, it was a little of both. He knew Frank was kidding. He was surprised that he was kidding too. It had been so long since they'd enjoyed any form of amusement together.

Rush gestured for Frank to join him on the rusty bench ahead. As they sat, the air stilled and noises from the nature swelled. It did feel somewhat supernatural. Maybe even healing. Frank couldn't remember the last time he had just sat and allowed himself to rest without giving in to self-loathing. With someone there, doing nothing felt, for the first time, like the one thing in the world that he should be doing.

'What did I tell you?' said Rush with the kind of charming self-satisfaction that reminded Frank of his mother. He hadn't allowed himself to think about her in weeks; it was too painful. Today, the idea of her pottering about in the kitchen, while Shelly or one of the others and their kids wreaked havoc on the place, made him smile. If he concentrated, he could hear her go-to phrase, 'Tap ya noise!' in the back of his mind.

'It's nice, Rush. Real nice,' he replied, closing his eyes and smiling to himself as the warmth from the sun above washed over him.

'Much better than col' col' London.'

Frank laughed, opening one eye a little as he turned to look at Rush.

'You could say that.'

Frank knew what Rush was doing but appreciated it all the same. Up there, in the two or three hours tucked away from their usual surroundings, trying to forget was easier. Not so easy that thoughts of the people he had left behind didn't lodge a lump in his throat – he couldn't focus on them without losing himself in guilt and shame. The light breeze on his face, the sound of birds tweeting in the distance and the comforting stillness of his cousin made the pangs of regret less pronounced. He was enjoying himself. He was thankful that his cousin had tried to make that happen.

Frank turned to study Rush, now leaning back with his arms interlocked against the nape of his neck, studying the landscape. He always had that sense of calm and quiet authority in his element – the great outdoors. As if the trees and birds and bees would bow to him if he asked politely – a courtesy he'd surely keep up even if he had otherworldly powers; he respected the earth that much. If Frank had never left Jamaica, stayed back with his grandmother, who raised him while his mother worked in 1960s Birmingham, Rush was the sort of man he hoped he would have become. A simple, honest man. A man who people turned to when they wanted help, instead of the sort of man who needed it. Frank exhaled loudly, half intending to get Rush's attention as he continued to stare down at the crops below. He didn't know what to say, but he wanted to at least communicate that he would have said something if the words had come. Rush would know what that look meant, wouldn't he? Would he? It occurred to him then that he hadn't ever voiced those feelings out loud, hadn't told him how grateful he was for everything. But where would he even start? As he readied himself, Rush kicked his ankle playfully.

'So cuz, tell me. What's so good about England anyway?'

Chapter Ten: The Return

(Jamaica, 1981)

A dozen trips around the world, and this one felt like the first. Mikey had let his camera lead him through paparazzo scrums in the streets of Milan, on trains through Northern Europe, through foothills in Tanzania and university campuses across the United States. But never 'home'. As the plane circled the runway at Heathrow Airport, the seatbelt restricting the flesh around his stomach, he felt he might as well be minutes away from launching into outer space.

Tumbling blonde curls released from atop the head of the middle-aged, sunburned woman next to him draped over his hand as she fidgeted with a noisy paper bag of hard-boiled sweets. He stared at the strands, sighed and flicked the bundle away, catching her eye. She smiled at him. He lowered his eyes and attempted one back, not wanting to offend, but not happy about how much space she was taking up either. He turned towards the window, willing the plane to take off, terrified that it would.

'First time going to the Caribbean?' a gruff northern voice said. He felt a finger poking his left arm and turned, perplexed.

'First time?' she asked again.

Her boldness angered and amused him. He shook his head in reply, content with entertaining her, for a moment.

'Not our first time either,' the woman responded, gesturing to the similarly pink-skinned, curly-haired Brunette woman next to her. He wondered if they were sisters.

'This is our – what, Jeanette?'

'Second time,' the other woman replied in a hushed tone, nodding her head as she studied the inflight magazine.

'Second time,' the blonde repeated. 'Well, to Jamaica. We try to go away every year, don't we? Somewhere hot.'

The brunette nodded. Mikey raised his eyebrows and attempted a smile.

'*Beautiful* place, int it?' She didn't wait for her companion to nod this time. 'But terribly *poor,* when you're not in the hotels, mind,' she whispered, leaning in as she elongated the word 'poor' and staring at him, as if waiting for confirmation that she hadn't said the wrong thing.

'Ooh, the *poverteh,*' the friend added, paying little attention as she flashed a photo of an expensive watch in the magazine to the blonde. Mikey cringed.

'Are you going for your holiday?'

'No,' he said. He'd have left it there if he could have, but he also welcomed the distraction. The plane was taking off now, and he didn't want to look down.

'I'm going back. Well, home. I'm going back home. For work. For – for now.'

'Ooh, I thought I could hear an accent. He's Jamaican, Jeanette,' she said, prodding her friend, who was now too busy studying a page full of pricey perfume.

'My neighbour was from Barbados,' the blonde woman added. Mikey bit his tongue.

'What do ya do?'

'Photography.'

'Photography!' the women replied in unison, pronouncing it 'photografeh', raising their eyebrows at one another.

He felt his cheeks burning. He was good at this, usually. It excited him to wade into other people's worlds for brief moments. To challenge them, or learn from them, or simply listen. He felt it made his photographs richer. Helped him to understand things he hadn't considered, or complicate things he had. But he hadn't picked up his camera in almost a year. And the longer he'd let his case collect dust since returning to the restaurant, the harder those conversations became. He could perform them, in part. But his interest in them was fading. He often lay awake at night wondering what else he was losing in the process.

'Chicken, or beef,' the air hostess asked with unsettling brightness. There were six more hours left on the flight and the sleeping pills he'd taken half an hour earlier hadn't kicked in.

'Chicken, and a brandy, please.' The women next to him helped pass the tray to his seat and went back to their conversation.

They'd given up trying to bring him in to their conversations about an hour before, only breaking the invisible barrier to flash him the odd knowing glance when other passengers did something of note, as if the three of them had developed a secret language. He was as grateful for their kindness as he was irritated.

Mikey struggled through his meal, a bland concoction of creamy meat pieces and potatoes and greens, a roll of bread, an aluminium-covered dessert he didn't want to touch, and knocked back the cheap brandy with ease. He asked for another. Gulped that down in no time too, eliciting whispers from the women beside him. It didn't take long for him to start to feel tipsy. Perhaps it was the sleeping tablets. His eyes began to feel heavy, drowning out the harsh lights above him as he gave in to the weight of sleep. Slipping in and out of a dream state, he felt himself falling out of the sky and into the ocean, the security of land just out of reach.

'Ladies and gentlemen, please return your seats to the upright position for landing,' a voice said from what Mikey briefly thought were the heavens. He opened his left eye and made out the blurred images of the two women next to him rifling through their bags. They smiled at him as he came to, the chattier of the pair bringing her shoulders to her ears in excitement. He felt happy for them. It must've been nice knowing they'd soon be filling their boots with sun, sand, sea; hotel food, drinks; maybe even a local market or two, where higglers would sell them trinkets for quadruple the price they could ever get away with selling to locals – who wouldn't dream of buying anything from them in the first place.

To these women, Jamaica was just a nice, warm, exotic place to relax. A place to forget the cold and gruelling slog of life in Britain, if that was their experience at all. He'd have been harsher on them were the job he'd taken on in aid of something else. But the truth was, rather than returning for good, or to rebuild his country, as he'd dreamed in his youth, his great return was in aid of that very thing: tourism. A dry spell of commissions and a lack of interest from the city's exclusive galleries had forced him to return to his parents' restaurant for far longer than he was comfortable with when a friend of his recommended him for a photography job with the tourist board back home. He leaped at the opportunity, wondering if, following years of having his work rejected, London really was the place for him after all. Not caring at the time that it was exactly the sort of gig he'd have refused a decade before.

How long Mikey would stay in Jamaica, he didn't know. But he needed a break from the eyes of suspicion and bewilderment gallery assistants and magazine editors would meet him with when he presented them with his work. He couldn't hear another person tell him 'sorry, we're not looking for artists at the moment.' Or, 'And what is your connection to the photographer who took these?'

Much as his younger self would have balked at the prospect of him 'selling out', at thirty-six years old commercial photography was the only way to give him some semblance of the living he'd dreamed of – and in the one place he'd ever felt whole. How far had integrity got him, really? Sweating in the kitchen at the family restaurant. Cynical and depressed, with dwindling friendships and a barely functioning love life.

They were disembarking now. Even from inside the plane, even at night, the heat was suffocating. He had been away so long that even the temperature, a climate he fantasised about when hailstones grazed his face, or fog filled the air, had become alien to him. He felt his body betraying him as sweat formed under his moustache.

The brief descent from the plane outside was nothing

compared to the heat in the actual buildings of Norman Manley International. Connecting flights from Miami and elsewhere had turned the small airport into a frenzy, with hot and bothered tourists and returning Jamaicans moving through mazes of queues in rapid succession. When greeted at passport control, he felt his accent thickening on his tongue. The uniformed, crisp-haired woman before him didn't seem fazed – a sign, he told himself, that he was blending in.

Once through the crowd, he stood stationary in the middle of it all, allowing himself to take it in, wondering whether he should take a photo. He started to walk backwards. A porter bumped into him, telling him to watch himself, 'nuh man'. Then a woman carrying a sleeping child kissed her teeth and cut her eye as she struggled to get by his frozen body. The curtness would have pissed him off in London, but he told himself it was because they saw him as one of them. Even if, as he soon noticed, it may have simply been because he was blocking the baggage-handling system for another flight.

With his bags in tow, he made his way towards the exit to catch a taxi. He was accosted by taxi drivers in an instant. In the glow of the evening moon and fluorescent lights, he puffed out his chest in a bid to hide his nerves and strode towards a casually dressed dark-skinned man, slight of frame, the least pushy of the bunch.

'Hello, sir, taxi? the man said, smiling. Mikey was offended at his formality. Apparently, it was more obvious than he thought that he'd come from foreign.

'Yeah man,' he responded, giving him the location, Duhaney Park, and details about it in the strongest patois he could muster. He was disappointed when the driver's eyes widened a smidge. Mikey couldn't tell whether it was in recognition, or amusement.

'Yes, breddah. Trow yuh bags in the back and mek yuhself comfortable,' the driver said with a smirk. Mikey may not have been back for a while, but he knew better than to get in without settling on a good price. He tried his rich dialect on again, gave it some bass, and asked how much. The driver gave him what he thought was a good price. Too good. They were halfway to his aunt's house, whipping around blind corners and inches away from other motorists, before he realised why.

'Hol' on, hol' on, hol' on,' Mikey said with increasing volume, failing to get much more than a flicker of eye contact with the driver through the rear-view mirror. 'No sah!' he bellowed, the driver's gaze fixed on him now. 'What's the price in Jamaican dollars? No buddah give me no tourist, US dollar price.'

The driver apologised, but was reluctant to relent, claiming, in breezy tones, that it wasn't up to him.

'Stop the car,' Mikey threatened, hoping the driver wouldn't call his bluff. He didn't want to try hailing a cab on the roadside with all his luggage, where he might have to go through all of this again. He repeated himself, staring the driver down through the rear-view, sounding more shrill than he'd intended.

The driver stifled a smirk and sighed.

'All right, all right.'

Mikey wasn't sure whether his tone had worn him down, or if he was too tired to argue, but he was grateful for the deal he was eventually offered. It was still more than he'd wanted to pay, but it was enough to make Mikey feel victorious. And then a little guilty. He could afford the higher price, even in US dollars. But it was the principle; he needed to be taken seriously if he was going to be here for a while.

Finding middle ground between his hard-man act and civility, he tried to break the ice with a few softball questions about where the man was from in Jamaica. How long had he been driving? Twenty years? Wow. And could he reach him if he needed a ride again? By the time they reached his aunt's, the pair had something of a rapport. Mikey wondered whether he still had the gift of the gab after all.

A wave of fatigue and exhilaration came over him as he arrived at his aunt Sarah's house. Mikey hadn't seen her since he was a child, but knew her voice well from occasional phone conversations in London. She was already outside, teetering back and forth in her pristine white sandals, by the time he shut the car boot and made his way towards her yard. When she embraced him at the white iron gate in front of her modest house, he felt – though every bit the thirty-five-year-old, and more portly than he'd ever been – as if he'd returned to his infant state. It was the warmest welcome he'd remembered receiving in years. Her sincere, moon-eyed gaze cut through him, filled him up with warmth. He felt instantly bound to her. Part of him wondered whether that feeling stemmed from something deeper – a soul bond forged through surrogate mothering. She'd moved in with his mother for a couple of years when he was a baby, grated him mounds of green bananas and nutmeg for his porridge as a toddler, his favourite to this day.

'Laad Gad, my *baby*,' Sarah exclaimed, beaming at the unshaven, middle-height, afro-haired grown man before her.

He wondered whether his face, though splashed with flecks of moles and marred by dark circles and a dimmed light in his eyes, looked the same.

'Yuh FAT, ee?' she said, slapping his back, making him squirm.

As she enveloped him in her fleshy arms and held him against the talcum powder on her chest, he could have sworn he shrank several inches.

So much about his aunt had remained constant despite all the years gone by. Her home; her cooking; the warbling, warm tones of her voice. Even the contours of her face put him at ease. Though not the spitting image of his mother, she bore enough of a resemblance to her that he felt Sarah had travelled with him. He was home. Finally.

As they broke from their embrace, a thick-limbed, chestnut-hued, cropped-haired woman, no more than twenty-five, watched on from her compact front garden with curiosity. He fixated on her pink, figure-hugging capri pants, and the suggestion of curves under her baggy, floral blouse as a gentle breeze lapped at her clothes. Mikey wondered who she was, and whether Sarah, who was busy trying to snatch Mikey's suitcase from his grip, knew her.

'Ah who dat?' Mikey whispered, gently snatching the handle from his aunt. Sarah playfully kissed her teeth at his insistence on refusing help, looked up and waved in the woman's direction, causing her to break out in a radiant smile. Mikey swore he felt his heart stop. Should he be waving too?

'Yes, darling. That's Anne. Nice girl. Helpful.' She snatched the suitcase back again. 'Anyway, yuh eat yet?' she added, pulling at his wrist to follow her inside. Mikey shook his head and began to follow his aunt's lead. He stole a look behind him, where the woman still stood, staring at him as if she knew all his secrets.

The sea breeze in Negril, where he'd travelled for work, was making Mikey feel nauseous. The heat was a straitjacket, the grains of sand beneath his toes cold and insecure, and the once soothing white noise of the encroaching waves was beginning to mutate into a grave roar.

He reached into his cargo shorts' pocket for his handkerchief, still fragrant with traces of VapoRub from the cold he'd had in England some weeks before, and blew his sweating nose.

'All right, yes. Nice, nice,' he called out with feigned enthusiasm, running his fingers over the damp edges of his cropped halo of hair, the same way he'd kept it since his adolescence.

Click.

He pushed down on the shutter-release a couple more times, capturing the pair of tanned white models sprawled out on wooden beach chairs before him. They flashed bleached grins and clinked glasses filled with food colouring, the silhouettes of poised Black servers just out of focus in the background.

It had been a couple of days of shoots like these, and with the water drawing nearer to the shore, this one was nearing its end.

'Tilt your head to the left a little, Mary. Henry, head up slightly,' he instructed, the glare from the sun glistening on his subjects' oily skin, and the horizon reflecting in the black lenses of their sunglasses as they made slight adjustments.

'Beautiful, beautiful,' whispered the creative director,

James, inches from his ear. Mikey paused and glanced to his left for a second, disturbed. The creative director let out a shallow cough and muttered more adjectives into the air. Mikey carried on shooting. James was a gangly, toned, brown-skinned man of too many words and a strong appetite for Yves Saint Laurent's Kouros perfume and unlit cigarillos. His beige polo shirt, caramel-coloured slacks and tan woven-leather shoes seemed too sensible for him, somehow. Something to do with his vacuous observations, perhaps, or his tendency to treat each shoot they'd been on as if he were witnessing an artist capturing a masterpiece, not a manicured ad for the Jamaica Tourist Board.

It was a scene that was supposed to connote luxury. A 'don't you wish you were here' moment to seduce nervous western tourists to 'Make It Jamaica Again' in spite of previous travel advisory notices. The election of the Edward Seaga administration the previous year had signalled a new lease of life for the tourism industry, which courted foreigners and embraced capitalism with more vigour than ever before, promising paradise, seclusion and service with a smile.

Mikey was nailing his employer's vision. It was his fifth shoot in the four weeks since he'd been back to Jamaica – the first time since he'd left some twelve years earlier. Aside from staying with his aunt in Kingston before travelling to Negril for work, the longer he stayed, the more it felt like it was his first time visiting. Like he'd dreamed it all up, the intricacies of the scenery morphing gradually as he passed through it. He felt ashamed of how uncomfortable it was for him. It should have fit like a glove. Not parts of it, not just when he was at his aunt's, but all of it.

They were losing light on the beach now. It'd soon be time to return to the lobby of the recently renamed Hedonism II, the flashy all-inclusive resort on Negril's picturesque Seven Mile Beach. He shook the models' hands without looking into their eyes and began to pack up his equipment with as little urgency as possible. Perhaps he'd get a minute alone to think.

Mikey dreaded the debrief that always followed these jobs. His eyes would glaze over as the creative director gushed, in his uptown accent, about how 'wicked' the photos looked, oblivious to the glare of the hotel's employees and guests as they ogled them, as they always did. Was he seeing it? Mikey often wondered. Perhaps he was ignoring it. Each time he'd search the man's gormless face for a clue, he came up short – missing half of what James had been saying to him in the first place. It was exhausting. He could feel his bed beckoning him from the other side of the airy lobby. Much as he hated the concept of these hotels, their beds sure were comfortable.

'Mikey!' bellowed James, backing up towards the path to the hotel. 'We'll catch up in a few, yeah?'

Mikey's heart took a nosedive at the thought. He nodded, sighed and turned towards the sea, where the descending sun had turned a terrible shade of amber. He walked towards it, letting the cool water lap at his toes. As a boy, this same ocean had filled him with wonder. It had burned him inside not knowing what lay beyond it. Excited him too. Staring out at the horizon and knowing exactly where it led made him sad for that child, and what might have been if he'd never left.

Mikey liked the way his body looked against Anne's when they lay together. Like deconstructed gizzada, he'd say to her in jest, making her thick eyebrows dance and the faint laughter lines on her rich, clear skin crease.

'Like who?' she'd always fire back with a gentle push. He'd lost count of how many times they'd played this game in the dozens of nights they'd lain awake since he returned from Negril. Him coming up with some inane metaphor for their lovemaking, her lapping it up. In the quiet of the night, the routine, their entwined limbs, felt the way things ought to be. He could be happy, he thought, if he never left her arms.

Since being formally introduced to Anne, his aunt's twenty-five-year-old neighbour, one late Sunday afternoon, he felt a duty to show her the best of him. He'd felt bad for staring blankly at her when he first arrived, and hoped they'd run into each other again. She showed up unannounced with fragrant fevergrass cuttings from her grandmother's garden across the square, a gesture that his aunt felt warranted tight hugs, a bowl of stew peas and an hour of gossiping in the kitchen. Mikey had been napping in the living room when she arrived. He was embarrassed when, after greeting her, he realised he'd missed some flecks of dried drool in the corner of his mouth.

It wasn't just her appearance that drew him to her, though it accounted for a lot. As time passed, he found himself opening up to her too. She was the sort of person who could draw poison out and relieve the body of pain with a look, or a few short practical words. With her, his shattered dreams felt less shameful, but instead, unjust. A wrong worth righting. No, that had to be righted. She'd got him to show her his work before he arrived in Jamaica – a collection of his proudest portraits, stashed in a folder in the lining of his suitcase before she encouraged him to make copies for her and his aunt. Who else had real-deal photographs of Ali? Who else could capture the spirit of a student movement or Caribbean funerals in a series of stills? She'd lit a fire in him. A desire to claim his stake in a world that didn't want him. And space to express how much he was hurting from waiting all these years to see it become a reality. Other women might have judged him for being a failure. Not Anne.

He felt more of a sense of duty to her in his absence from her. Even at work. Even when around other women. Especially around other women. Mikey's charm had come back to him in full force. He'd had months of practice with models and the like, and picking up work for the Jamaica Information Service had introduced him to new faces. Being busy and having an excuse to put on a show was beginning to make him feel good about himself, even if the stories his photos accompanied were PR fluff for an administration he despised. He washed away the bitter taste of guilt with drinks from open bars at events he attended, rubbed shoulders with public figures and police chiefs he quietly resented, and made keen women feel like the only people in the world, boosted by the security of having someone good, truly good, at home.

Fantasising about Anne and a life together somewhere down the line was one of few things that made him feel like he was doing all this for a reason. He'd come home to her every few weeks just for the reminder. It was why, some days earlier when alcohol has been coursing through his body on the way back from a boring dinner he was working, he felt a foreign urge to make things official. It had only been a few months, but he'd never felt so safe, never so sure that this was the person he was meant to be with for the rest of his life. He wanted her to know how serious he was, short of proposing. As the taxi pulled closer to the drive at home, he wondered whether he should seize the opportunity to say as much. The soft glow of the side lamp in Anne's window let him know that someone was up. With her grandmother in Portland for the week, her original hometown, it had to be Anne. Mikey smoothed down his moustache and checked his breath. Not great – but not offensive, either. He'd have to stop himself from sprinting to the door once the car stopped, he was sure of it.

'Yuh wan drop off here?' the taxi driver enquired.

Mikey was about to nod, when a shadow approached the door to Anne's and disappeared inside. He squinted, wondering if he'd imagined it. He rubbed his eyes and answered the driver without making eye contact, peering closer at the closed door. Were those two shadows he could see? Or one? Maybe her grandmother's trip to the country had been cut short. Perhaps he was seeing things.

As the figures grew faint, he jumped out of the cab and shut the door, forgetting to pay the man.

'Excuse me, excuse me – sir!' a muffled voice boomed, followed by sharp, rapid taps on the window that made him jump. Mikey handed the man the cash – more than he'd wanted to pay – and thought about whether to just go back to his aunt's. Talk to her in the morning. It was probably nothing.

He approached his aunt's door and held the key in his hand, staring down at it as if it had the answer he was looking for. No. He was being silly. He'd dropped in on Anne like this many times before – and she was always happy to receive him. She'd do the same now. He turned back and began the short few steps to Anne's door and knocked harder than he'd intended. A curtain in the window of a neighbour's house twitched slightly. The people dem round 'yah too inna, he thought, sick of the watchful eyes in the local area, where everyone seemed to know everyone else's business. He knocked again, softly this time. She didn't usually take this long to answer. Was she sleeping? He waited for what felt like five whole minutes and almost gave up. The crash of something falling kept him in his place. He knocked again.

'Coming, coming,' Anne's faint voice hissed. She sounded put out. Maybe she had been sleeping. Mikey tried to ignore the pang of guilt that ran through him and moved closer to the door.

It opened to reveal his lover in her dressing gown. She didn't look tired. Just a little vex. Confused, even.

'Mikey . . .' she said, staring at him.

She looked beautiful, even with a face like thunder. The faded rouge on her bottom lip accentuated the fullness of her mouth. He wanted to kiss her. He leaned in to do so. She pulled back, still not leaving enough room for him to enter. He searched her eyes for warmth and found them frozen.

'Yuh nah guh let me in?'

Anne didn't say anything. Couldn't look at him. Mikey stepped forward and found his torso greeted with Anne's outstretched arm. He wondered what he'd done to offend her.

'Not tonight, Mikey. We'll talk tomorrow, okay?'

Mikey didn't understand. They'd been on great terms just days earlier. Nothing, at least on his end, had changed since then. He lowered his head, trying to hide the disappointment on his face. She caught it in her hands and whispered some assurances about there being nothing wrong. It felt like she was lying. He hated himself for doubting her.

Accepting defeat, he removed himself from her grasp and took a step backwards. She smiled at him from her firm position by the door and began to shut it. In the gap where she had been standing, he noticed a pair of large black-and-white trainers he'd never seen before. A bitter, burning taste began to form in his mouth from the back of his throat as one of his mother's favourite expressions echoed in his mind. *Trouble nuh set like rain. Trouble nuh set like rain. Trouble nuh set like rain.*

He felt dizzy, the houses around him looming like jan-crows. He was convinced all the curtains were twitching. All the neighbours gathered to watch his heart break in real time. Part of him wanted to knock on the door again to confirm his suspicions. A larger part couldn't face it. As he started towards his aunt's door, the quaint square he'd come to love appeared a shrinking cell. He felt himself itching at the walls of its confines, desperate to escape the tainted memories he'd made. Bursting into the house, past his sleeping aunt and into his bedroom, he knew the only thing he could do now was to leave.

The morning after their awkward encounter, the air between Mikey and Anne had shifted. She didn't call on him like she normally would. When they did bump into each other, she averted her gaze and lowered her voice, keeping things brief, as if she were being watched. He didn't bother asking her whose shoes he'd seen, or why she was so hostile.

They both knew the answer. There was someone else. It was an unspoken horror that he'd forced down within him the moment his suspicions were confirmed. She didn't deserve to know that. She didn't deserve to know him at all. Not any more.

Weeks later, the pain was still palpable. He'd see Anne in his dreams with her faceless lover every night, then be confronted with her in the flesh on venturing out of his auntie Sarah's house. That she still had said nothing killed him. It was the coward's way out. He wasn't sure how much longer he could withstand it. Work, though, was a welcome enough distraction. There was always the possibility of getting his own place, somewhere far from here. Away from the whispering neighbours, and Sarah's insatiable curiosity about why she hadn't seen Anne much these days. He emptied his heart of passion and his mind of thoughts, instead, hobnobbing with bosses at JIS and taking on more photography side quests that neither inspired him nor entertained him. He wondered what his hero, James Van Der Zee, would think of him now. They'd met once at one of his exhibitions in Harlem when his hope was still fresh and dreams were still in reach. The Harlemite's quietness had shocked him, given how loudly his photos spoke to him and so many others. If he'd known then that he'd be embraced with wider arms in there than he'd ever experience in his birthplace or hometown, he would never have left. Now that coming back home had failed to make him whole, he knew he had to leave this place, too.

Chapter Eleven: The Flat

(London, 2007)

What happened didn't seem possible until it was happening to her. Sure, she'd been aware of the dangers. Planned for them too. She understood people didn't care about the fate of women like her. But she'd been so careful in the past. This guy was supposed to know better – he was their landlord.

'Shit,' she thought, her body cold against her as she held herself. 'Maybe this was on me?'

She closed her eyes tight to shut out the idea. No. Being attacked was the result of bad luck and worse people, a chain of indifference and abuse so long and pervasive that it ran like veins through the body of society. It was because of *him*. Because of *them*. She was just doing her job. That's what Lawrence would have said. She winced as she realised she was still there, in that house, blood from the side of her head soaking into the cotton mattress protector on the bed beneath her, a thin off-white rectangle that barely covered the discoloured lattice pattern of the dirty mattress below. What would Judith say if she knew?

The prospect of judgement made her wince almost as much as the pain. Almost. Parts of her skin felt tender, blemished by the force of his fingers in her flesh. She felt white-hot pain in so many places she was too scared to inspect herself. Had he broken anything? Had he left anything intact? Where was he?

The precise moment when she knew she was in danger was still repeating in her mind. Where was he? A clip show of nightmares. The way the force of his grip had left markings on her skin, the sharpness of his breath in her nostrils. How her legs collapsed onto one another in a heap when he hit her.

She'd had this client before. Somehow, amid the fear and disgust that consumed Judith whenever she was forced to acknowledge Lisa's work, the idea of familiarity had been comforting. 'William?' she'd ask whenever Lisa set out for work. The suggestion being that, if he was the one housing them, if he hadn't pulled anything odd in the past, he certainly wouldn't in the future. Lisa knew how naive that was. But it was a smart system too. It had, until now, kept her relatively safe from harm, hadn't it? Everything that she could rely on to feel safer when working had been meticulously planned. She'd even begun talks with Shirley about pooling their clients and working out of their friend Lawrence's flat. Once they had enough, they'd move out and leave Delroy in the dust, working on their own terms. Lawrence did this work too. He made enough through camming, bouncing and escorting to keep the flat but he worried his landlord had grown suspicious of him and how he made a living. He needed distractions. He knew what he needed to do.

Lisa first met Lawrence at a queer bashment rave in an abandoned warehouse in what felt like the middle of nowhere. He noticed, though she didn't stand out, that she'd been dragged there against her will. The way she crossed her arms over her chest, only letting parts of her body catch the beat at first. The light that washed over her when she found the courage to move from the sidelines to the middle of the dancefloor, among sweaty, free bodies as she pelted her waist into a frenzy. The surprise in her eyes, when she marvelled at what she had let herself become a part of, screamed: 'I've never been here before. But as God is my witness, I will be here every single week, sweating through every pore, from the dead of the night until dawn.'

Lawrence often told her he remembered that feeling well, knowing, for the first time, that he was right where he was supposed to be. He'd said he wanted her to linger in it, let her feel all the good, her body floating just above herself all night, thankful for the high. They often reminisced about when they'd first met. The idea that they hadn't known each other all their lives already felt strange after a couple of months. Each had other friendship circles, yet theirs had felt like the reawakening of a dormant memory. They made sense of things together, painted a fuller picture of themselves. Him, to her, a gateway into a world she had shut out, a protector she'd never had. Her, to him, a comrade and a reflection of his younger years. He wanted to nurture her in ways he hadn't been when he arrived in the UK as a child, after over a decade without seeing his father, his surviving relation. She was happy to be nurtured.

Lisa remembered how that night, when he realised he'd been staring at her and she had been staring right back, smiling and snaking her back to the beat, Lawrence wined over to her, shuffling his heels and waist as he travelled sideways.

His skills made her screw up her face in delight, dabbing her sweat rag over it in a playful, rhythmic manner. They danced all night long. Smoked all night long. Laughed, even cried. It was one of those bonds that seemed inevitable – so strong that Lisa had forgotten all about Shirley, who'd been busy pushing up against Delroy all night, only breaking away when the mostly Black crowd amped her up for having enough rhythm – for a white girl – to get by without ridicule.

'So, what have we learned tonight?' Lawrence had asked on their walk to the bus stop in the early hours of the morning, scalding-hot chicken and chips in hand. Lisa's laugh had been hearty and bright, like a child who'd been taught to cuss, egged on to repeat the words out loud for the first time.

'Anybody who tink seh dem need fi worry bout what MI ah do? Go SUCK yuh BUMBA RASSHOLE!' she'd squealed in delight, the alienness of the aggression fresh and cool as mint on her tongue. When Lawrence learned a few weeks later that Lisa, like him, dabbled in sex work, he was sure their connection was fate.

'Where do you usually meet?' Lawrence asked, once they'd both pulled the truth out of each other.

'At our flat, sometimes hotels,' she said, shuddering at the thought of her last client's watchful eyes on her body – their landlord William's eyes. His rough hands chafed like sandpaper against her delicate skin. He was friendly enough in the sense that he knew his pleases and thank yous, but being around him felt chilling. There was something missing in his eyes. He was becoming more daring about ignoring the terms that had been set.

'Wanna come use my flat at some point?' Lawrence had

offered. 'I can feel my landlord teetering on the edge of evicting me for being too sexy. If you want somewhere that's safe, clean and doesn't come with a lingering pervert, let's talk. I bet a woman or two would calm his nerves, stop him fantasising about sucking my dick. You know, keep him guessing.'

'About you being gay?' Lisa had said, clasping her hands over her mouth in regret – she hadn't meant to sound so surprised.

'Yes honey. If it's a possibility that I'm not – shocking, I know – he'll back off. Trust.' Before she'd had much time to think about it, Lisa had agreed.

The arrangement had worked the first time they tried it. Lawrence, when he wasn't working, served as security, his strength screaming out of his biceps. He was intimidating when he didn't speak – particularly to non-Black clients – and his face was stern, not the puddle of warmth it melted into when he was relaxed. The clients respected him. Feared him. It was a good plan.

Now, in the plush, soulless surroundings of William's home – where was he? – she wondered why she'd taken this job. Delroy had pressured her. She should have refused coming to his house. But she hadn't. Now it was too late. One thing she'd done, minutes after arriving, was text Lawrence a hasty 'Something off. Keep eye out', when William brought something up about a 'change of pace' and wrapped his hands almost tentatively around her throat. He was trying out a more dominant side, apparently, pushing her around slightly, and laughing as he did so. It didn't feel like roleplay. He'd made a discovery. He was thrilled. Her fear was turning him on.

She remembered making her excuses and heading to the bathroom to text Lawrence. Something told her to unlock the back door she passed on her way. If something was wrong Lawrence would need to get in. The sight of a large Black man forcing his way into a home on this street wouldn't do either of them any favours. She coughed as she turned the key to mask the sound and beelined for the bathroom, already drafting the follow-up text instructing Lawrence to make his way to the back of the house. No time. She'd been in the toilet for one minute when William shouted, telling her she was taking too long. Her clammy fingers trembled as she tapped the send button, her phone unresponsive because of the moisture. 'Coming! Give me two mins,' she'd shouted back, trying her best to sound normal. What the fuck was wrong with her phone? Could she make a dash for the back door? Did she even need to? Lisa told herself she was overreacting. She took a deep breath and glanced at her twisted face in the mirror, told it to relax. Try again. She took her phone to her thigh and rubbed it against the fabric of her trousers before tapping the send button again – gently, this time. Before she had time to check whether it worked, the bathroom door swung open.

Lisa clutched her head and tried to piece together the rest of what happened. She had tried to fight, but whether she was successful . . .

A car started and pulled away in the street below. Lisa attempted to pull herself up out of bed before the pounding pain forced her horizontal again. Head spinning, she let out a groan and squeezed her eyes shut. She held her hand over her pelvis and lingered. She wanted to assess the damage but she was afraid. She couldn't bear to touch herself; it would be excruciating if she did. She lay there, wanting to be anywhere else. Where was he?

A voice said, 'Lisa.' It was coming from inside the house. She stopped breathing. He was back. She needed her phone. Had the text sent? Scrambling with her hands, she searched the thin sheet beneath her for a rectangular bulge. Nothing. She'd have to get up, no matter how much it hurt. Hoisting herself upright, she peered over the edge of the bedframe and saw it peeking out on the floor beneath. As she grabbed at the cracked screen with her fingers, she made out an unread text from Lawrence. She struggled to bring the phone – which now felt like it weighed ten pounds – closer so she could unlock it. It wasn't recognising her face. Was it really so disfigured?

'Lisa!' the voice hissed again. 'Lisa!' – it was getting closer. She thought how ridiculous she'd been for deriding the prospect of dying a boring death in the past. Nothing sounded more lovely now. She closed her eyes tighter, waiting for the worst the world could offer. As the heavy footsteps approached, she steeled herself to the new pain that was coming. He reached her bedside faster than she expected. His jacket rustled as he went to move one of his limbs – probably his arm – towards her. When it landed softly on her face, she opened her eyes. It was Lawrence.

'Lisa, baby. We have to go. Now. I fucking laid him out, but he could wake any time.'

Lisa started to cry. She couldn't make sense, but she put her arms around her friend's neck and allowed herself to be lifted. She wasn't light. But she felt like a baby in his arms.

'We're going to the hospital, okay?' he whispered.

'I don't want . . . No hospitals, please.'

'But baby, your head. We don't know what kind of damage—'

'Please. I'm okay. I think. Let's just go back to yours for now. I don't want you to get into trouble. Did you drive?'

'Car's a street away. Look, we'll go back to mine for a sec but promise me you'll let me take you to get looked at today.'

'Fine,' she said, gesturing for Lawrence to put her down. They were by the back door now. A barely conscious William lay slack-jawed in the corridor. He moved slightly. Lisa froze. Lawrence kicked him.

'If we're going to a hospital, we're driving far away from here first.'

'What about Judith? What are you going to tell her? Shit, Lisa.' The worry in his voice made Lisa feel guilty. He had just saved her life, and here she was arguing, forgetting about those closest to her. They hurried to his car, neither speaking until they'd driven away.

'Sorry for being like this,' she whispered, looking down at her body like it was rotting.

'Don't, Lisa. You don't have to call anyone until you're ready . . .' Lawrence's eyes darted, searching to have her face reality, without scaring her too much. He indicated and turned a corner smoothly, the car's clicks and revving sounds filling the silence.

'Judith lives in that flat with Delroy, Lisa. Do you think it's going to be safe for her if he finds out? When he finds out?'

Lisa's gaze was on her lap. She was picking up her fingers one by one, letting them fall onto her left thigh with light taps as she tried to transport her mind further from herself.

She didn't like Lawrence's line of questioning, practical as it was. It made her feel responsible – for what had happened to her, for what could happen to the women because of her – to Lawrence too. In the fog she was trying to lose herself in, there was no room for that. Lawrence insisted.

'You think he'll trouble her? I can tell her to meet us if you want. We can even pick her up. She's working now, right?'

Lisa nodded. She could feel Lawrence looking at her. She felt like a child.

'Then St George's it is. We'll get you checked out, we'll call Judith and then we'll take it from there. You can stay with me for as long as you want. Judith too. I'd leave it a bit before checking in with Shirley. We don't want her to think something's up. Delroy would pick up on it in a second.' Lawrence turned to look at Lisa. She might disappear if he didn't check.

'Do you ... remember what happened?' he asked, looking at her for longer than he should have, causing the car to sway momentarily and swiftly eliciting toots from a spooked car near him. His anger turned towards the sky-blue Nissan Micra.

'Yeah yeah, we're all trying to get somewhere!' he bellowed at the wide-eyed driver, shouted a hearty 'fucking cunt' and sped off.

'Sorry. I didn't mean to—' Lisa's lips twitched upwards slightly. She was smiling, almost. Lawrence reached out a free hand to stroke her shoulder. She sighed.

'After I went to the bathroom to text you ...' Lisa let go of her fingers and looked up to focus on the scene outside. She wound down the window, letting the cool air consume her. There wasn't enough room to breathe in here. She inhaled, exhaled and grabbed Lawrence's knee before continuing, still looking away.

'He'd ... amped himself up or something. We hadn't started anything yet, but he was ... puffing up his chest, trying to push me around, all that.' Lisa recalled how the act, from a usually timid William, had almost made her laugh at first. Some of her more vanilla clients had stumbled across kink and acted brand new in attempts to escape their blandness. But they'd always asked first. Nervously laying out what they wanted to try. She was great at appeasing those clients, pretending a tentative spanking had made her writhe in agony. But William's eyes had been sinister. Though awkward, there was a newly discovered confidence behind his gaze.

'He ordered me to go to the bedroom, I – I remember that. He wanted me to be scared, or something, gripsing me up everywhere, trying to hurt me enough to prove that he'd go further. It wasn't working ... until it was. I don't know what happened after he hit me. I can't remember. I was trying to get away.'

Lawrence had pulled into the hospital car park while Lisa was talking. What could he offer now that wouldn't feel insensitive?

'I heard you scream when I came in. Do you think that was when he hit you?'

Lisa shook her head. She couldn't remember.

'You were fully clothed when I got upstairs. He had you on the bed ... and you'd gone limp. Your head was bleeding. All I could think to do was create a diversion in the hallway at that point. As he came out, I—'

'I don't want to relive it, Lawrence,' said Lisa through closed eyes. Her tears were falling down her cheeks now.

'We won't talk about it. I'm sorry.' Lawrence took his hand off the steering wheel briefly and wiped a tear from his eye too. 'You're safe now, you're safe.'

Lisa spaced out again. It felt as if she were on autopilot. Bustling, then sparse, then busy-again streets whizzed by in streams of colour and blended sounds. She would have to tell her cousin the truth. She couldn't tell the doctors, though. The fumes of the petrol from the car made her feel terribly, horribly sick.

Chioma, the woman she'd been dating for months, had called three times before Lisa checked her phone. The relationship – Lisa's first 'real' one – was the best thing that had happened since the night she met Lawrence. It made sense. It terrified her. She protected it from everyone, even those who would understand. She couldn't call her back now. She'd hear the fragility in her voice, know something was wrong. She'd try to help. Lisa couldn't handle her lover seeing her traumatised. Their relationship was where it needed to be. It had to stay that way.

She was a world away from the tender, cosy world they'd forged.

They had met at Black Pride that summer. She had Lawrence to thank for that too. He'd dragged her along, adamant that she wouldn't regret it. When they entered the small crowd of people – dressed in the garb society stuck its nose up at, dancing, laughing, drinking, organising – she knew he was right. All she could feel was awe. She moved through the bodies with care, weaving through as Lawrence dipped and slipped ahead, both uncomfortable and more at ease than she'd ever been in her life. Passers-by brushed light fingertips on the small of her back, calling her pet names, their eyes gentle and glazed over from the drink, or whatever. They seemed happy and free in impossible ways. Let it rub off on her. Transfixed, she lost sight of Lawrence for a second, spinning around in a panic and hoping to find him towering above everyone. She bumped into someone. A slight-of-frame, pink-afroed vision. As the person moved towards her, returning her gaze, she felt pinned to the spot.

Judith was also on the missed call list. They always talked at around 11.30 in the morning, when Judith's supervisor went on a smoke break, and Lisa indulged in her daily brunch ritual. She couldn't eat before 11 – it felt unnatural. It was 12.18 now. Judith would be busy. Lisa didn't have to worry about calling her back for an hour or two. But there had also been a call from back home. She hadn't spoken to her mother since she'd left, but it couldn't have been her. She lived on the opposite end of the island, in Saint Thomas. Some cousin asking for money probably, their boldness bolstered by the myth that Lisa, like other UK-bound relatives, was rolling in it.

The fluorescent tube lights in the waiting room burned her eyes. They'd been travelling for an hour and a half and wanted to sleep. It hurt to move her gaze, let alone her head. Perhaps William had done damage. She felt a hand caressing hers and strained to look down. Lawrence was stroking her, cool metal from his thick gold rings on his deep brown fingers soothing her. She ran a finger over tiny, wiry hairs on his scarred knuckles, and smiled. He'd come just like he said he would. Lisa started crying.

What had started as dodgy accommodation in a dingy flat had morphed into an endless stint in a holding cell of sorts: bare and uncomfortable, overseen by a man with a thirst for power and a compulsion to wield it at random. She'd never talked to Shirley about it. They didn't have to. When they were working, they were working. When they weren't, they were avoiding what was obvious in the flesh-penetrating look that would come over Delroy whenever Lisa was forced to squeeze past him in the hallway. In the hot whispers he'd breathe onto the back of her neck while she made breakfast. The flushed red of Shirley's cheeks when she'd caught a quick glimpse of him scraping his calloused thumb against Lisa's jawline as she sank into herself. What had started out as 'favours' for Delroy turned into routine. It was the only thing that placated him. What was a little fondling now and then if it meant she'd avoid his ire and earn a little more?

It hadn't always felt so oppressive, Lisa thought, as memories of her initial 'run-ins' with Delroy began to come back to her. She saw the dirty, middle-aged loser of a man for what he was before she started working for him. Handsy. Unpredictable. More of a threat to Shirley than her. When their 'talks' began, she realised how intelligent he was. He could sell plane tickets to birds. Even convince you to sell yourself. The most recent talk was no different. She had come home drunk after a night out with Lawrence, expecting an empty flat as Judith had gone to visit some church friends in Reading, and Shirley was out for the night. Shirley's absence usually meant that Delroy – the jealous type – would follow after her, to keep tabs nearby, or to ruin her night, daring anyone who glanced her way to fight him. He was home this time. Waiting. For what, she didn't know – but she had a feeling. He'd asked her to work 'with' him the week before, knowing she was desperate for money. She'd declined, respectfully. But faced with growing debts and with the courage of intoxication behind her, she felt herself bending. Nothing else paid enough.

His body language was expectant and unfazed when she walked in. He was sat lounging on one of the wooden chairs in the kitchen as rings of smoke unfurled from his brown, pillowy lips. Lisa smiled at him and began to walk towards her bedroom, hopeful that she might avoid an unwanted conversation with him. She wasn't scared of him exactly; he seemed to reserve his blows and passion for Shirley. But she didn't enjoy being alone with him. His lustful eyes, low and piercing, told her from the minute they met that he was attracted to her. How naive she'd been to assume that it wasn't all connected – the propositions to sleep with him, followed by propositions to sleep with clients.

'Baby love,' she heard Delroy call, just as she'd passed the kitchen door. 'You going to bed already?'

Lisa tried to dispel the chill travelling down her spine as she made her way back to the room. What the fuck did he want now? Picking herself up, like a child who knows they're in trouble, she entered, avoiding his stare, and took a safe spot near the fridge, just far enough away that he couldn't reach out and touch her. Would he do that, if he had the chance? He busied himself with rolling a blunt. He'd convinced Shirley and her to do things with other men. Why not him too?

'You been out on the town, then?' said Delroy, manipulating

the roach of his joint in between his index finger and thumb. Lisa nodded and smiled.

'Proper party girl, innit?' Delroy laughed to himself, licking the paper and rolling the brown and green mass into a thick cylinder between his fingers. Lisa said nothing. He passed her the blunt and she drew in the bitter fumes with gusto, making herself cough. 'That's right girl, get it into your lungs,' he laughed, slapping the table as she struggled to compose herself.

When she'd calmed, the softness of Delroy's face struck her. He'd be quite handsome if he wasn't who he was, she thought, wondering if it was the drink, pills and weed talking. Delroy patted the empty chair next to him and pulled it out so that it was directly facing him. Lisa took a seat and attempted to make small talk, daring herself to meet his eyes as she did so, thinking it might get her out of things faster. Though he was responsive, the smirk on his face grew more intense with each question, almost like he'd been tipped off about winning a prize. He asked if she was struggling. Maybe she was ready for the extra work he could easily provide.

'What?' Lisa asked, leaning in, surprised that she was still in the room, let alone entertaining the conversation. Delroy ignored her and licked his lips without breaking eye contact.

'Are you ready?' he repeated, almost sternly. She let him linger there for a second, wondering what to say. Some part of her curious about whatever would happen next. Delroy slid his hand to the top of her bare thigh, like rough stone sliding across silk. She was still wearing the maroon jersey bodycon she'd worn to the club, but felt as if she was wearing nothing. Her eyes followed his hands to her knickers – beige-coloured shapewear she'd assumed no one would see that night. She exhaled heavily and opened her legs further, knowing the drill. He struggled to slide his fingers past the taut elastic around her thighs, the barrier exciting him.

'Tell mi fi stop,' he said heavily, looking into her eyes as she pulled herself forwards, so the pressure of his fingertips was firm against her. She let him finger her until she pretended to come. When he was done, he shoved three fingers into her mouth, smirking again as she sucked the taste of herself and whatever else, keen as she could without gagging. She hated performing for Delroy. He still thought she was attracted to him.

'Go on, gweh. We don't want the Mrs finding out,' he laughed, dusting himself down.

'We'll talk money and ting in the morning. Mi have a nice gig fi yuh with William.'

Flashing a wink, he stood up and walked out, leaving Lisa alone in the kitchen with her shame.

Delroy had been exploiting her for so long she barely noticed the stakes getting higher. A few mumbled words and a pull on his cigarette and he'd persuade her to accept lower rates, loan her out to friends, make her meet men in shitty hotels. She learned not to go to those appointments alone. Lawrence had volunteered to become her unofficial security, waiting for signals via text in nearby cafés, or, depending on the establishment, in hotel lobbies, while she worked. She didn't always need him, but knowing he was near was a comfort. She'd request an extra hotel key before her appointments, slipping him a spare as she walked in the opposite direction, pretending not to know him. Eventually, having him there felt necessary. She'd pay him sometimes for his time, even when he tried to refuse the money.

It was an arrangement she kept from Delroy. Something about his taste for roping people into schemes made her cautious. His request next morning, after their kitchen encounter, to visit the landlord in his own home, proved his lack of vigilance. William put a roof over her head but he was in no way trustworthy enough to be visited without Lawrence lurking around the corner.

It took a while to figure out why Delroy had such a hold over William. The landlord's bookshelf was stacked with fat books about politics and war, and biographies of former Conservative Prime Ministers, some she'd heard of, others she discovered after flicking through the blurbs. He shopped at Daylesford Organic and Waitrose. His house, laughably monstrous compared to their flat, was on a leafy hill in one of the poshest bits of Tottenham. She hadn't known it even existed. Why would he spend time with Delroy except for an ugly, nasty need?

Lawrence had been stroking her hair for a minute or so before Lisa realised he was doing it. Normally when she tuned out like this, he'd ask her where she went. No use in that now, he already knew. He changed the subject.

'So, my love. Ms Judith,' he suggested, hoping Lisa wouldn't shut down. She needed family here. Real family. Wary as Lisa was about admitting to what she did for a living, or worse, coming out to her cousin, she couldn't go without that woman's support. They were close. Lawrence saw, after meeting her a couple of times, that Judith cared, even if she did ask whether he was a 'batty bwoi' when she thought he couldn't hear her. At least she looked embarrassed when Lisa glared at her in response, daring her to go further out of line with a simple, 'yes, and?'

'I can't deal with her right now, Lawrence. She'll just make me feel more guilty,' said Lisa, thinking about the logistics of having her cousin there.

'*Guilty?* Baby, no one is guilty. Well, except those fucking men. I just want to make sure you don't try to deal with this alone. I know what you're like.'

A doctor interrupted them with an update about medication for the head wound. With fresh stitches and reassurances that she'd heal in no time, she felt marginally calmer. She hadn't told them what happened. Dealing with the police would have been too much. She didn't want to provoke Delroy more than she had. If she snitched on top of assaulting a client, what would he do? What if he took it out on her? She felt dizzy.

'Can we leave?'

Lisa didn't remember the trip to Lawrence's flat. She had woken up groggy on his lumpy spare bed, the sun burning her eyes, as if examining her yet again. She had no idea what time it was. She recognised two voices in the corridor. She could move her head more now, though it still hurt.

'She's not going to take it well,' Lisa could just about make out. Chioma was here, then. Lawrence must've called her. She thought she'd be angrier, but she wasn't. Not at all. Just embarrassed. Chioma walked up to the room. She had a dutiful, determined look about her. Her red-brown skin crumpled into a hopeful frown of sorts, her brown eyes squinting and her brown lips hiding gritted teeth. She was a mess, Lisa thought, almost amused at the serious demeanour she'd taken on, like she was going to fix Lisa and everyone there with sheer sincerity.

'Baby!' Chioma's eyes widened when she said it. Her pace quickened too. As Lisa recoiled, more out of shock than rejection, Chioma slowed her step and relaxed her face, kissing Lisa lightly on the nose, forehead and both cheeks.

'I came as soon as Lawrence called. He was only trying to help,' she said, looking into Lisa's eyes.

'I know,' said Lisa, reaching out for Chioma's hand, wanting it more than anything, surprising herself.

'We don't have to talk if you don't . . .' Chioma trailed off, her gaze drifting over Lisa's body and some of the visible stitches on her head.

'Fuck that,' she continued, angry at herself. 'Do whatever feels right for you. Talk. Don't talk. Shit. This isn't about me.' Chioma took back her hand and held her forehead, then put it back quickly, not wanting to make Lisa feel rejected.

'You're overthinking it, Chi. And you're right. I don't want to talk about it now. I don't want you to see me like . . .' Lisa looked down at herself, causing Chioma to shake her head. A kind of silent, 'don't you dare', which Lisa appreciated.

'But I will talk about it one day. And I'll be . . . myself again one day. I think.' She tried to stem the flow of tears with the back of her hand. They kept coming anyway. 'If this is too much, I get it. It's been what, eight months? You don't have to do this for me, Chioma.'

'I want to.' Chioma smiled. 'And I think you need to tell Judith too,' she added, turning Lisa's expression sour.

'About the attack? Really? Then I'd have to explain about my job, Shirley, how I managed to swing it with Delroy that

Judith would be living in that flat with me in the first place. She might never speak to me again.'

'You said once that she was the kindest person you knew.'

'Yeah, right after I told you what she called L. What she *calls* L when she forgets herself. Even how she's looked at me when you've come round.'

'Look, didn't she make him the best brown stew fish he'd ever eaten? Doesn't she share a room with you?' Chioma added, ignoring her.

'Jesus, Chi, the bar is proper low for you, eh? One good piece of fish and everything's out the window.' Chioma raised an eyebrow and busied herself with rearranging Lawrence's dog-eared coffee-table magazines.

'It's not low, it's realistic. I know plenty of "cousin Judiths", babe. I lived with mine, remember? But look, Judith *knows* you're gay. She's just too uncomfortable to bring it up.'

'Too disgusted, you mean.'

'That too,' Chioma replied, laughing.

The thought of Judith knowing who she was made her heart sink, though a part of her had always suspected it. She'd never been good at keeping a secret. Head hanging, eyes closed, she whispered:

'You – you think she *knows* knows? Like, for real?'

Chioma dropped her head and raised an eyebrow.

'Yes, babe. She's smart, that one. If you think she's going to abandon you after this? You're wrong. She needs you as much as you need her.'

Lisa wasn't so sure. Despite Chioma and Lawrence's urging, she took her time before deciding to tell her older cousin about the attack, instead crashing on the other side of the city with Lawrence for the night, pushing her fear deeper until she thought, for a moment at a time, she could no longer feel the full weight of its presence, until the black, tentacled memories crept back into the forefront of her mind, threatening to take over when she slept, or when things had gone quiet.

Chapter Twelve: The Job

(Tottenham, 2007)

When a private number flashed on Judith's screen that after-noon, she thought twice about answering. She'd been in the middle of her weekly cleaning ritual, scouring the bathroom skirting boards so hard that she'd chipped some paint off. No matter, she thought, inspecting the beige marks. Better uglier than filthy. As much as cleaning pained her when she was at work – which, as Shirley had prophesied, was beginning to dry up – wiping and hoovering the flat down, especially when she had it to herself, felt cleansing.

'Lard God this place nasty,' she said out loud, as if she'd been waiting months for the privilege. It felt good to say. Every inch of that place had been soiled with bad memories, some preced-ing her arrival, no doubt. She wanted to do her best to mask the lingering stench with bleach and lemon-scented products. As her phone vibrated along the floor, she glared at it for a second, a part of her hoping it wouldn't be about another short-lived gig, a gig she desperately needed if she was going to make rent this month. She'd almost rather work for Delroy. Almost.

Judith picked up the phone and let the person on the other end do the heavy lifting. They'd called after all.

'H-hello?' a man's raspy voice on the other end enquired.

'Hello,' Judith replied sternly, still scrubbing dust from awkward corners around the perimeter of the room.

The voice on the other end of the phone kissed his teeth and muttered something about 'damn technology', followed by incessant tapping and the sound of dial tones. It appeared he didn't realise she had picked up. Judith shook her head.

'Betsy!' he bellowed. The voice sounded like it belonged to an older Jamaican man. Confused, yet intrigued, she continued to listen, amused at the farcical exchange she could hear in the background. Betsy, she assumed, judging on the faint sound of a woman replying in the background, was a little too far away to be of use, drawing out exasperated grunts from the man. Was this a relative? Judith resolved to help.

'Hello? Hello sir?'

'A who dis?' the voice barked.

Judith stopped what she was doing, a little taken aback by the man's curtness.

'A who *dis*?'

Though the man couldn't see her disapproval, it was made crystal clear by the silence on the other end. They'd got off to a pretty bad start just thirty seconds in, and neither were sure of who they were actually talking to.

'Oh!' the voice exclaimed, a tinge of shame in his voice. He continued, distracted, 'I'm looking for a Judith. She did umm, apply for the management umm, position.'

Judith's heart began to pound. She was thankful she hadn't hung up. Always right on time, He's always right on time, she thought as she brought her eyes to the ceiling, in thanks to God.

'Oh! The job!'

'Yes. Mi— I thought I'd got the wrong number, sorry. My phone, it nuh work so . . .' the man trailed off. Judith waited for him to continue. 'I'm Mikey, the owner. Betsy said you did a good job in the interview. So we want you to come in for trial shifts this weekend coming. Okay?'

Betsy. She had spoken to a Betsy at a restaurant she'd sought work in some time ago – a pipsqueak of a girl. Pretty. Small. A comically high-pitched voice. Judith had forgotten she even applied. When she'd walked into that place two months earlier, it had been on a whim. That day's catering job had been atrocious – too few staff, too many rude clients – and she needed to believe that there was something better, just for a little while until she finished her course in a couple of years' time. She'd fantasised about becoming a nurse back home. She could have called herself one. She cared for both her parents through their old age, washed their baby-soft, cracked skin until it was time to put their bodies to rest beneath the soil. She'd looked after her sister and her brother-in-law too, helping to position his body when the professionals couldn't, so he didn't feel too much pain in his limbs because of the polio. She was passing her modules with ease. She read books on nursing gifted to her from what she had thought was her well-to-do Londoner cousin Lisa. When those were done, she read them again, or watched medical dramas late at night, closing her eyes and envisioning herself in the scrubs, tending to people quietly, while the doctors stole the show up front.

A job in a restaurant wasn't in her field, and it wasn't her dream. But it was something she was certain she could do for longer than a day without coming close to leaving for home again. She approached the upkeep of everything in her life with medical precision. Running a restaurant – a small Jamaican restaurant with a tiny menu – would be no different. She would keep it spotless. Make sure regulars were met with a smile. She could keep up with the bookkeeping (she'd always been a whiz with numbers) and, when necessary, she could keep people in check too. If the chef was sick or couldn't make it in, she had a damned good palate and a knack for working under pressure too. How she'd learn to get along with that rude man on the other end of the telephone, however, was another issue. Maybe he wouldn't be in as much as the others. He was nowhere to be seen when she'd gone. Judith closed her eyes tight, the mole under the left side of her face disappearing into the faint grooves around it. She took a deep breath in, exhaled and replied:

'This weekend is perfect. Yes. I will be there.'

After some less than enthusiastic mumbling from the man about timing – Mikey, did he say his name was? – it was confirmed. She would be in at 7 a.m. sharp, and she was not to be late, a warning she had to stop herself from kissing her teeth at. 'Punctual To A Fault' may as well have been her last name. She was forever barking that same order at others. But this man, Mikey, she said to herself so as not to forget again, didn't know her. She couldn't blame him for taking the precaution. A part of her respected it. Judith put the phone down and steadied herself, smoothing down her clothes as the news sank in. She put away the cleaning supplies in the hallway cupboard and let her body rest against it. It would be no picnic for her feet, but if it went well, this job could be the start of something.

She remembered the day she walked into that restaurant like it had been last week. She'd just worked a gruelling catering gig, the first job she was able to secure without the help of her cousin, and it was getting dark out. She was reeling from the smug indifference of those glassy-eyed guests at the corporate event – a financial services award ceremony for teefing money, probably. They looked through her that night as they always did. Enough to tell her when to stop pouring wine, or to top it up, but not so much that she'd ever have the privilege of being met by their gaze, or their gratitude. She felt duppy-like at those gigs. Wondered whether, if she stood perfectly still, the guests could pass through her body. She needed to get out; she had no choice but to stay.

Shirley was always telling her how fickle the 'gig economy' was, how quickly opportunities could slip out of her hands if she wasn't smart.

'Listen, Judith love,' she'd come to call her. 'Whether your boss is making you hand out crusty old beef to a bunch of wankers or setting up dick appointments for a crusty old wanker, the work is shit,' she'd say. 'But I can tell you this now, that zero-hours waiting by the phone crap ain't going to be your ticket out of here.'

It seemed like a cruel, short-sighted warning at the time: take bad, precarious jobs for survival, but don't get stuck in the endless cycle of thankless labour – how was she supposed to do that? What had refusing jobs like these done for Shirley? What had they done for her cousin Lisa? The ability to turn down legitimate shifts they didn't want to do for illegitimate shifts they also hated? She agonised over that conundrum on the bus home, the soles of her tender feet pulsating so much she thought they might bleed over the lining of her thin, black dolly shoes. No solution ever came to light. As grateful as she felt to have the option of not working for Delroy, the alternative was wearing her body down with each standing twelve-hour shift. Then she saw it.

Often as she had dismounted the bus and shuffled past the job-ad-riddled bus stop on the race to get into the shower, that night, for whatever reason, she stopped before a fluorescent green piece of paper with the name CUDJOE'S in big, black, block writing. It was a front of house opportunity for a Jamaican restaurant in Harlesden. Full-time. An hourly rate almost double the £4.50 an hour she was currently getting. Under the harsh glow of the off licence behind the bus stop, Judith reached up and ripped the flyer from the tape that had fixed it in place. If the job wasn't already filled, she'd at least make sure she was the last local applicant to get in touch. When she rang the number minutes later, and by some miracle the position was open, she'd headed down to the restaurant, blistered feet and all.

Discarding the warm, soapy, discoloured bucket of water beside her into the toilet, she began to hum as images of her new potential life rolled out in an idealistic montage across her mind. If she worked hard enough, perhaps she could afford to leave tasks like these behind. Live in a nicer flat, with clean, freshly-painted walls that didn't have years of neglect caked into them. Maybe she could even swing her cousin a job. Perhaps she could swing her a job there too, in time.

Lisa had called to say she was staying the night with Lawrence, a man who made Judith laugh, even if he did carry himself the way he did. Better him than one of the others, Judith thought.

When Lisa came the next evening, she brought Chioma and Lawrence with her. Judith thought the Antiguan-Nigerian woman polite. But she made her uncomfortable too. Her 'boy clothes', as she thought of them, were loud. The first time she'd swung by the flat to take Lisa out for lunch, Judith couldn't help but stare. Everything about her felt wrong. A needless cry for attention. She was a striking girl. She didn't need that costume Lisa insisted was just her 'being herself'. Her eyes were kind, framed by long, natural eyelashes that were visible even from a distance. Her sharp jawline could have belonged to a catwalk model. And her cropped afro hair, which she'd dyed blonde and shaved a parting in, could have looked beautiful, if presented in another form. She was a proper Londoner; Judith could tell by her accent. But her heritage was immutable. She broke out into patois on occasion. Talked about visits 'back home' as if she'd ever lived in either of her parents' respective countries. Sprinkled foreign words – Yoruba, Lisa said it was – into her speech on occasion and ate mango the 'right way' – tearing the skin with her teeth, devouring its flesh without making a mess and leaving nothing but a white, polished pip when she was done.

The brightness of their smiles when they were around each other took away from that. They looked at each other like protruding pieces of meat from the pot – ripe for plucking.

Judith would come home after Saturday morning shops to find the pair closer than friends usually were, or basking in the yellow sunlight streaming through the kitchen window, Lisa beaming while stirring a cup of something steaming and Chioma delivering jokes Judith didn't understand. What good friends, Judith often forced herself to think, the lie a momentary comfort in the face of something so unnatural.

She remembered the first time she heard the name Chioma. Judith was used to seeing Lisa carelessly applying makeup before 'going to work'. But the first evening she noticed her enjoying the process was an evening when the pair were due to meet up. Lisa had called her a friend. And Judith had thought nothing of it. Perhaps she was just excited to be going out. So excited that she'd decided to deviate from her usual little black dress and blazer combo, donning a chartreuse midi A-line dress, with an over-sized diamante statement necklace, and a belt and blinged-out shoes to match, even after Judith hit her with a judgemental 'Ah dat yuh ah wear?'

This new 'friend', apparently, appreciated that kind of fashion. She wondered at the time whether the rumours that had long circulated about her cousin back home were true. They'd never talked about it, but it seemed an all but confirmed fact. Lisa's story about how they'd met – in church, which she'd never seen Lisa attend – had never quite added up. When Lisa returned looking dishevelled and broken, she wondered whether the woman had done something to her.

Lisa's head had been hanging so low Judith feared it might break clean off. Her limbs so slack in Chioma and Lawrence's arms that she looked like she might collapse.

'What's wrong?' Judith made her way towards the trio in the hallway of the flat and searched their eyes for answers. Lisa was sobbing, though she couldn't see her face properly. She attempted to lift her chin. Lisa recoiled and turned her back, making instead for their bedroom.

Judith could feel her blood pressure rising. What sort of depraved things had they all been up to? What dangers had they exposed her to?

Lawrence took Judith by the hand and led her to the living room to sit on the sofa. Chioma, sheepish and sad, shuffled closely behind.

'Judith, is he here?' he asked in whispers.

'Ah who "*him*"?' Judith looked around the room, confused, realising he meant Delroy. She shook her head. 'No, him nah here. Weh wrong with Lisa? What did you two do?'

Chioma and Lawrence sighed in unison. Judith was getting scared now. She called out to her cousin, but got no response. It was unlike Lisa to ignore her beckoning. Chioma took over from Lawrence, placing an unwelcome hand on Judith.

'She's just going to have a little nap. Is Shirley here?'

Pulling her head back in disbelief, Judith manoeuvred herself out of Chioma's way and walked swiftly to the bedroom. Her cousin was lying on her side on the futon, staring. Her eyes bloodshot and glassy. Her face bruised. There were stiches in her head. Judith's heartbeat quickened.

'Auntie Judith,' Chioma said from behind, reaching out to touch her shoulder once more. 'Let's let her rest for a bit. We'll explain everything.'

There was a ringing in Judith's ears that hadn't subsided since she heard the words 'Lisa' and 'assaulted' in the same sentence. It grew louder with the revelation of more ugly, horrifying details: Delroy's part in it; Lawrence's heroic act; the hospital; the unanswered conundrum of where, if anywhere, they would be safe. She knew something like this would happen. She blamed herself for not putting her foot down. For being seduced by the live and let live nature of this blasted city. This country.

By the time Shirley returned home, the agonising story relayed to her in front of Judith, the ringing had given way to a pounding headache. What if Delroy came back? What if he'd returned the night before? What if he'd done something to Judith and Shirley in everyone's absence? She felt sick. She wanted to go back to a time when none of this was her reality. When coming here was an idealistic pipedream.

'Delroy's phone has been off since yesterday,' said Shirley through tears. She hadn't taken the news well. The groceries she'd been carrying slipped out of her fingers on hearing what had happened, smashing a jar of Dolmio pasta sauce on impact with the floor. She took to cleaning in a frenzied, unhelpful manner that snapped Judith out of her trance and into care-taker mode. She led Shirley's daughter Megan out of sight and into the bedroom she shared with her mother. As the child followed and began to play, Judith's heart broke. Shirley's crying and shouting was ringing louder in the background, something that didn't seem to faze her daughter. Looking down at the oblivious child from the doorway to the small bedroom, she thanked God that the child didn't seem aware of anything amiss. She busied herself making figurines soar through the air with her tiny hands, whispering 'whoosh' as she did so. Save for her light-brown skin and curly brown hair, she was the spitting image of her mother. Judith hoped, in the trajectory of her life at least, they'd share no further commonalities.

Lisa was still sleeping in the bedroom. With outbursts and shock exhausted for now, the group had moved in silence to the kitchen to discuss the logistics of what to do next, ignoring the sense of unease that had crept over all of them with the knowledge that none of them was safe, not really. Cups of tea, made dutifully by Lawrence, had gone cold. But the presence of the mugs seemed to comfort everyone. As they took it in turns to react, they'd cup their palms around them, ting fingernails against the ceramics, or stroke the smooth surfaces, soothing their restless hands.

'If he knows about what's happened, he won't come back here any time soon,' Shirley said after some back and forth about whether they should hole up in a hotel, or out of the city for the time being.

'How can you be so sure?' Chioma snapped, her emotions taking over her relative resolve.

'His papers.'

'Yuh mean, him nah have him stay?' Judith said, cradling a sleeping Megan in her arms. Shirley shook her head.

'I'm sorry,' said Lawrence. 'But what has that got to do with anything?'

'Del is slick. Probably one of the smartest people I've ever met. But he's shook of any kind of authority you know. Freezes when sirens go off near him in the street. It's like he thinks they can smell the crime on him. He's been living here illegally since he got here. I'm surprised you didn't know.'

'Me and 'im nuh talk, Shirley,' Judith muttered under her breath, irritated at the suggestion that she'd know much of anything about that man.

Shirley began to offer apologies, as if assuming responsibility for him. For all of this. It crushed Judith in a way that surprised her. She tapped a tentative pat on Shirley's arm, hoping it would reassure her.

'So, your solution is to what? Go to the police?' Lawrence was too agitated to pay much attention to the awkward dynamic before him.

'Of course not. But we can make him think we will. William too.'

It was a balm, sure, that something could threaten Delroy's return, Judith thought. But it felt too tenuous. What if he called their bluff? She hadn't seen in him the intelligence Shirley and Lisa mentioned. Just reckless, pure evil. She shook her head, catching Shirley's eye.

'Trust me on this.'

'Mi nah know, Shirley. Yuh keep tell me "believe me" this, an "trust" that, and look weh happen to . . .' She gestured towards the room where Lisa slept. 'Mi cyaan do this . . .' Tears began to roll down Judith's cheeks. She looked like an entirely different person. Smaller. Younger. Fragile. The three other adults in the room got up to comfort her, wrapping their arms around her, surprised she was letting them. When they broke their embrace, Judith was attempting a smile. She nodded at all of them in gratitude, even allowing Shirley to wipe away the tears still streaming down her cheeks.

'Sorry. Let's do it. Mi just . . . scared.' Judith blew her nose and cleared her throat, willing the emotional spell to end. She knew her fear wasn't unique. They were all terrified. Devastated.

'So, what about his papers then?' said Chioma. 'I'm not gonna lie, the idea of reporting anyone to the Home Office isn't exactly . . .'

'Nah bruv. Let's report the motherfucker,' said Lawrence.

The foursome laughed for the first time in hours. Cursing, even to Judith, felt appropriate. But not too much more. She returned the child to her bedroom and lingered in the hallway before returning to her seat in the kitchen. Shirley was still going.

'No, really. I think this could really work. He knows William was beaten up by someone. That we have some kind of muscle on our side.'

Lawrence raised a finger to object, the worry on his face far more visible than it had been when he first entered the flat. Judith found herself worrying about him too. He'd been through a lot today.

'Let me land,' said Shirley, more curt than she'd meant to sound. 'I'm telling you, Del's a coward. He don't fight.'

'Unless him dealing with women,' said Judith, surprising herself.

Shirley nodded, unfazed.

'Look, seriously, we just need to let him know what we're prepared to do and he'll fuck off. And we can work William too.'

Shirley appeared agitated. Transfixed. She was clearly running on adrenaline now, the grief of discovering the worst simmering under the surface. Even so, she'd never seemed so sensible to Judith. She could feel a budding sense of respect for the woman and her ability to think clearly in the face of so much adversity. Getting rid of Delroy might work after all. But what of the silent landlord at the centre of all of this? Couldn't he just seize the flat from all of them? Call the police on them too? Shirley squeezed Judith's hand and tilted her head forward.

'Delroy has a lot on William. Too much for William to go to the police. And I, believe it or not, have a lot on both of them. I think there's a way out of this that may mean we can keep the flat – and get rid of them both. For good.'

Lisa was leaning against the kitchen doorframe. Her hair was out of place and her loose nightie hung off her slumped body, making her appear boxy and child-like. They hadn't noticed her presence until she gasped in reaction to what Shirley had just said. Chioma rushed over to her and caressed her face. Judith would have felt uncomfortable in any other circumstance. But she could see how much more at ease her cousin became following the embrace.

'If this is too much,' Chioma began, following Lisa's lead as she took the fifth seat at the kitchen table.

Lisa closed her eyes and exhaled, placing her fingertips lightly on her girlfriend's wrist, as if to tell her she was okay. She outstretched her palms on the table and looked each one of them in the eye.

'Shirley, what were you saying about how we could keep the flat?'

Chapter Thirteen: Cudjoe's

(Harlesden, 2007)

When Judith first prised open the heavy, flyer-infested door to Cudjoe's, Mikey felt a change in the air. He'd been shelling pistachios as the counter – a pet peeve of his staff, for they were forever cleaning up after him – and debating with his new decorator, Frank, at the table opposite about whether Gordon Brown was indeed going to make a good Prime Minister. As far as Mikey was concerned, he wouldn't. 'It'll be more of the same. Mi nah care if him Labour or whoever, the white people dem will continue to look out for themselves no matter who's in power, y'ear?'

It was a spiel Frank had heard about ten times since he'd picked up work at Cudjoe's that summer. First, a request to redo the interior, now painted a bright green colour that old Cudjoe himself – Mikey – had chosen against the advice of everyone he asked. Later on, odd jobs here and there, some light plumbing, a little electrical work. Frank had learned to say nothing and nod along. It was easier. Debate led to Mikey pulling out some obscure reference to his political activism, or veiled threats to stop hiring him.

Mikey was ranting when Judith walked in. She had slicked

her natural hair back into a low bun, the sheen from her hair gel and the sun outside lighting up her middle parting like an airstrip in the night time. She wore no makeup, save for an inconspicuous brown lipstick, and a couple of coatings of mascara – her version of the full works. She wasn't either of the men's idea of a bombshell in those clothes, and at her age. Yet the curves in her stout body, and the grace with which she moved, even when struggling with a heavy door, was alluring. Her face, though twisted into a grimace because she'd been rushing, was kind. Her brown eyes shone in the sunlight, and the flecks of small moles and beauty marks at the top of her cheeks were unusually beautiful, even if her asymmetrical face wasn't conventionally so. As she walked into the restaurant, the rest of her outfit gave way to a stronger reaction from the two men before her, though she still had no idea why. She was wearing bright blue pedal-pusher jeans that hugged her thick thighs and high backside; some sensible, small silver hoop earrings; and a boxy black T-shirt that she'd tucked in at the waist, the jersey fabric pulling against her very large breasts, her skinny ankles like petrified sticks in the Umbro trainers she'd purchased for the job. She didn't worry about looking pretty at the best of times. *Pigs*, she thought to herself as she felt the men's gazes. *All men are pigs.* Judith wouldn't have worn the outfit, but after showing up in a brown suit with leather loafers last time, she now knew better. Judging by the reactions of the two men, she wondered whether she had indeed made the right choice.

'Can I help you, miss?' said Frank, grateful for the break from Mikey's incessant moaning. Setting his bowl of cornmeal porridge aside, Frank stood up from the table and wiped the corners of his mouth as he approached the austere woman.

'I'm here for the trial shift? For the manager position,' Judith said modestly. Frank looked over at Mikey – who had returned his attention to the pistachios – and back at the woman before him. 'Mikey, yuh nuh ear the lady?'

Mikey perked up, embarrassed at being caught again with his head in the clouds – a sign of his age, he worried. Brushing pistachio crumbs off his clothes, he hopped off the stool with a little difficulty and clasped his hands together, mouth still half full.

'Yes, 'ow can I 'elp you, Miss . . . ?'

'Judith.' She reached out her hand to shake Mikey's, recognising his gravelly voice as the rude man on the phone. He shook it back, still a little confused. This inability to listen was an ongoing problem of his, she thought, catching the younger man's eye behind him as she smirked to herself. As Judith's stony expression softened, Frank returned the smile. Without saying anything to each other, they seemed to be on the same page about Mikey.

'Ah yes, for the trial shift,' Mikey said, eventually, ushering Judith to a table behind Frank, his eyes lingering on her as she walked past him. As the pair sat, Mikey filled Judith in on the ins and outs of the place.

'No breakfast after 12.30. When the food done? It done. We put a likkle aside for some of our regulars, though. You'll get to know them as you get used to the place.'

Her hours – if her first day went well – would be from 7 a.m. until 4 p.m. She would be expected to stay on top of staff about cleaning, do a bit herself, check on food supplies, handle orders, sort the rotas, run the place in Mikey's absence. All things Judith could handle with ease. She had worked at her aunt's restaurant in Portland for years. The system was slightly different here. It was nothing she couldn't deal with.

Mikey had noticed how well his new hire was doing just two days in. Between serving as a new friendly face for the locals, and dramatically improving day-to-day operations – including introducing a ticketing system for orders at lunch and dinner time – she slotted in like she'd been there from the start. It was the sort of military precision he admired in his mother. Better yet, his grandmother back home. After five minutes, Judith had won the hearts of colleagues and regulars. Some asked after her once she'd left for the day. And he found himself thinking about her too.

Mikey opened Cudjoe's because he knew the business. If he didn't love it, it was work he could stomach to earn a living after his photography career dissolved into nothing in the late seventies. Stranded in Jamaica with barely enough fare to return home after his first visit since he left, he'd returned to work with his parents in west London. This was after a year or two of working for the Jamaican Tourist Board, a stint that he blamed for his financial misfortune, losing decent pay and a yacht because – as he told it – he'd been overlooked in favour of some white American photographer called Bob.

'They supplied him with a helicopter, a four-star hotel. He brought two assistants down. They were paying him five thousand dollars a day for that campaign,' he'd tell anyone who made the mistake of asking about the history of Cudjoe's. 'They were taking the piss, absolutely taking the piss. I just went to them and said, "I'm fucking fed up" and left. Haven't looked back since. Going back home was one of the biggest fucking mistakes of my life.'

Cudjoe, or Mikey, depending on how well you knew him, had made something of himself before this, so his story went. He'd snapped film stars across Europe, captured the essence of Britain's burgeoning Black communities, rubbed shoulders with the political elite.

'It all started from that shitty Retinette camera,' he'd say to whoever was listening.

You learned to listen and nod along. Questions like 'and what happened next?' were welcome. Anything deeper was not. Not even Judith, Mandy and Frank, Mikey's closest friends, knew whether his stories were true. Had he really been on the cusp of fame? Capturing images of Stokely Carmichael in Paddington? Travelling Europe? Being personally thanked by P. J. Patterson for his contributions to Jamaican culture? It seemed unlikely. There was little evidence, save foggy testimonies from the odd old friend who'd visit Cudjoe's. If he'd been so successful, so prolific, why hadn't he made it? newbies might enquire.

'I was a talented Black photographer in the sixties and seventies. They didn't believe I took the dyam photos,' he'd reply. 'And besides, the teefing woman of my dreams just trow all my shit out the fucking window one day. Most of my work is long gone.'

Between failed relationships and the elitist photography scene, Mikey felt he was owed. No one knew what he'd done in the years between returning from Jamaica after that tourism gig. They just knew he'd landed on his feet. That, as far as Mikey was concerned, was all they needed to know. His days of squatting in different places around the country were a fog best forgotten. He shuddered when he thought about the places he'd lived, the conditions that over time became normal to him.

His core belief had been that he'd escape the fate of his parents, docile failures who'd swallowed the lie of the British Empire then shrivelled up and died when it revealed itself to be a sham. Yet he couldn't help but note that by his mid-thirties, his father had had a successful business, a wife, a child, a home, a life. At thirty, Mikey had nothing but a plate-washing job and story after story, the words gibberish the more he repeated them. When the opportunity to take over the small Italian restaurant in Harlesden that he'd been working at as a porter, then a waiter, then a supervisor, and finally, manager, came up ten years later, he snapped it up without thinking. Something in this world was going to be his, even if it was just the modest dream of his father. If Mikey's bitterness and jealousy became tiresome, his charisma could make up for it.

He was often a joy to be around. People gravitated to Cudjoe's because of the food, yes. But it was the character who'd coolly greet them that was the true pull. It was why it didn't matter when Mikey had his trusted decorator Frank paint the walls a sickly shade of lemon-lime, clashing dramatically with the white and black chequered linoleum and bright red furniture. Nor that the food service often operated under a first come, first serve policy, delivered with either a grin or grimace, telling customers at the end of a long day that 'no, we nuh 'av dat'.

Between Mikey's electrifying smile, a grin that made his eyes disappear and his cheekbones rise, and the atmosphere – the constant bass of reggae, samba, soca, soul – it was a special place. Youngsters and local thinkers had even taken to holding weekly meet-ups there, discussing the plight of the Black community in Britain, or back home, wherever 'home' happened to be. He liked to be in the mix of things, offering wry asides for his audience-cum-clientele as he absentmindedly polished surfaces.

Judith and Frank's work meant that Mikey, over time, worked less. The food was covered by the three-person team of chefs, the counter service by Ivy and Judith and the upkeep for the last four years by Frank, who treated Cudjoe's as a second home. As often as they clashed, Mikey knew that he couldn't do any of it without them. He made no effort to get involved in their personal lives, keeping their interactions firmly in the restaurant. He'd show appreciation through an understated warmth. When Frank's last partner kicked him out for the third and final time, Mikey let him crash for a couple of nights. Frank had called mid-argument, attempting both to salvage his relationship and seek help, as his long-term on and off girlfriend (and the mother of his first two children), Gina, lobbed his clothes at him. Mikey could barely make him out between the less-than-convincing pleading from Frank that 'beah-beah, nuttin' a gwan', and Gina's retorts of 'fucking wasteman' and 'get out!', but he knew better than to hang up at the time. Frank had called him for a reason. He needed support – and by the sound of it, a place to stay. Much too private to offer up his own home – a cosy, yet chaotic maze of a place that only Mikey could navigate successfully – he offered an old camping bed in the basement of the restaurant. Frank showed up half an hour later with a sleeping bag, pillow and rucksack. Turned out his latest indiscretion had been revealed that evening when a woman called the house looking for him.

'She bloody hit the roof, Mikey.'

'I'm not surprised,' Mikey replied grinning, brandishing a set of dominoes and a litre of rum. He let Frank sleep in the basement for a solid month that time, joining him some evenings for a drink.

When Judith came to work shaken, exhausted and with red eyes, after a couple of months on the job, he slipped her a note with the number of a friend who was looking for a new lodger. He'd heard her on the phone in the stairwell a couple of times, crying about some man called Delroy who'd 'done it again', or the fact that Shirley didn't use a washcloth, 'so how she wash her dutty rass?', or Lisa's loud gay friend, who whooped and hollered while she was trying to revise in the living room.

'Your home should be a sanctuary. If you ever need some-where to escape, Cudjoe's is always here', read the note Mikey placed in her hand as he passed her from behind the counter, lingering a little, surprising himself. He took a seat by his usual stool and cracked open a bottle of malt, wanting to give her enough space to read the note, but not so much that he couldn't see the way her eyes widened and then softened as she digested the sentiment. She folded the paper into a tiny square and placed it in her front pocket, muttering thanks and meeting his eyes for just long enough for him to wink at her. He opened up the broadsheet he'd been using as a coaster for his drink and used it as a shield, obscuring the giddy grin that was trying to escape across his face, unaware of the amused yet perplexed look that had taken over Judith's. They had more encounters like these as time rolled on, their interactions laced with a sense of a softness and familiarity reserved, it seemed, purely for each other. Even her gentle scolding, in response to for his mood swings and dry retorts, felt sweet. Her smiles and gentle nudges dangerous. His weekly phone calls with her, a ritual the letter had allowed them to fall into, a lifeline. He could feel himself coming out of himself every day. It was terrifying.

As much as he talked the talk, it had been decades since Mikey had picked up a camera. He'd tried to forget about it, the part of him that saw his surroundings as art in the making, but it was ever-present, a constant burning in the pit of his stomach that feigned disregard only fanned. It felt more like an inferno these days. The same feeling he'd got when he went home for the first time, unaware of how disappointed he'd be when he left. Had he not learned from that terrible mistake, he'd have slipped right back into his old habits, dousing the fire with the click of a button, as if regret wouldn't inevitably follow.

Instead, he obsessed over the photos he had taken. The ones he'd hidden from himself. The ones that, in the earliest hours of the morning one day, sent him rummaging through piles of hoarded boxes in his modest, colourful flat. Consumed by curiosity, he was shocked by how quickly he happened upon a collection of photographs he'd vowed some thirty years before never to prise open again. There were black-and-white images of members of his old community in Notting Hill, small children smiling in the then-impoverished streets of west London, a white woman embracing a Black man outside the 'Pisshouse Pub' on Portobello Road as passers-by walked in the background. Faces he'd long forgotten, others he remembered like he'd seen them days ago.

Without thinking, he grabbed the box and opened the door to his flat, bolting outside, where he stood bathing in the yellow street light, wondering what had pushed him and whether he could stop it in spite of himself. He checked his wristwatch, a simple black Casio Judith had bought him after tiring of hearing him ask 'ah wah time it is?' every twenty minutes. Two a.m. He kept going, going, sprint-walking his beefy frame towards his car with a little trouble, daring himself to drive to Cudjoe's. He knew how far-fetched some found it that he'd taken photos of B. B. King and Sugar Ray Robinson in the sixties. What if he put the evidence right in front of them?

He was driving down the A3 to the restaurant before he knew it, taking in the nightlife like he was stalking the streets with a camera, looking for inspiration. Something was awakening. As he lifted the shutter to the restaurant, he imagined framed blown-up photos of his work all around the venue. His Blackness had meant the posh galleries and prestigious museums wouldn't accept him. But at his own restaurant, he could display his work with pride. Maybe. He dumped the box onto one of the tables, overturning a napkin holder with the force, and began to go through it, the expectant faces of his subjects gazing up at him, or off to the side at someone off-camera.

Mikey began to sob. A deep, gut-wrenching groan that

felt foreign to him. He couldn't remember the last time he cried. He felt hot at the idea of moving past this point. He didn't know what he wanted to do with the photos now that he had dug them out. A part of him did want to show them off. Despite being unsure of what he would do, he knew that bringing them here was the first step. For now, the best place for them was the basement.

On the wooden stairs and into the largely unused space below, he felt a sense of relief. Setting the box on top of a broken chair in the far-left corner, he circled the room. It felt right, leaning into his instincts in this way. Knowing those photos were down here would give him a boost that he didn't know he needed, he was sure of it. As he reached for the light switch, Mikey turned around to glance at the box one more time. As he flipped the switch and the room became awash with darkness, he smiled and said: 'See you again. Soon come.'

Chapter Fourteen: The Takeback

(Tottenham, 2007)

Getting Delroy to leave for good was the easy part. After changing the locks, reporting him and making sure word got back to him that the women had gone to the police, rumours began to circulate that he had left the city altogether. The flat immediately felt lighter, communal areas like the hallway, kitchen and living room no longer minefields you'd dash through in the hope of avoiding him. Bedrooms and bathrooms no longer holding cells. It felt like a home. A family – almost. It hadn't occurred to any of them that the tension that bubbled between the women would clear as swiftly as his departure came about. But the after-effects weren't gone entirely.

A month after the incident, William had agreed to hand ownership of the flat over to the women in exchange for their silence. It wasn't surprising how quickly he folded, given how nervy he tended to be about his wife and children even knowing he knew Delroy. Their arrangement had been long, but the foundations of their relationship had not been built on mutual respect. Despite procuring women and drugs for William for years, Delroy's rants to Shirley about that 'fucking eediat' who didn't know who 'him ramp with, to bumba', were unending. Being forced to meet the man in the back entrance of the house, in the dead of the night, when the neighbours couldn't see him, hurt his pride. But it was subdued enough through yet more cash, personal dirt and photos to blackmail him with, many of which he'd sent to Shirley.

The real clincher, though, was something none of them had been aware of. In efforts to find more dirt on him, Shirley, Lawrence, Chioma and Martin, Shirley's friend from the bookies, had dredged up more than they bargained for. In the diary section of a national paper, there he was, pictured hobnobbing with a former Conservative cabinet MP. They'd stumbled on more ties after the revelation: his donor credentials, his former life as a political advisor. He was enough of a someone that public knowledge of his transgressions would ruin more than his marriage.

Unsure as to whether he'd seen Lawrence, and with a desire to keep some distance between him and the women, the group thought it best to deliver the ultimatum through Martin. The negotiating stalled at the start – William's textbook arrogance blinding him to the gravity of the situation. Then, out came the photos. William guffawing, mid-speech, at a table racked with discarded magnum bottles, baggies and lines of cocaine; William with his head resting on a scantily-clad Black woman's shoulder; William raising his middle finger next to a smirking Delroy, staring down the lens of the camera. It didn't take long for him to fold after that. He offered money first. Tens of thousands to never speak of this again, to anyone. A visit to his home in broad daylight made him a little more amenable.

Martin, a middle-aged, olive-skinned, salt-and-pepper-haired white man, felt a sense of pride in being able to show up for Shirley like this. He'd never had a relationship with a woman like this. Someone he could truly call a friend, someone he'd do anything for, without the expectation of anything romantic ever unfolding – unless, of course, that was what she wanted. Having her respect, making her laugh, helping her to feel safe, had always felt like reward enough. Whether at the bookies, in quiet pub sessions when Delroy had been on one, or now. He'd taken pride in being the one to get William, an extension of Delroy's cruelty, to break. He'd slipped into the man's grandiose house one Saturday afternoon, the door unlocked because, as luck would have it, they'd been throwing a kids' party of some kind. He entered the house to find most of the adults spilling into the large garden beyond the grand sliding glass doors at the end of the airy open-plan living room and kitchen. Children in fancy dress were running about, ignoring calls to 'slow down, Arthur' or 'watch out, India' as they sent bubbles and squeals into the air. Martin didn't exactly stand out; almost everyone there was white too. But instead of the light shirts, neutral corduroys and brogues, his jeans, T-shirt and trainer combo gave him a slight enough edge to be noticed. He made his way confidently through the crowd, helped himself to an aperitif and made for the garden. William was leaning back, cackling with a man who may as well have been his twin, just beyond the crowd. Martin perched on a brick wall directly opposite them, staring at William with the intention of being noticed. It took all of a couple of minutes for the man to look up, widen his eyes and attempt to quell his internal panic. Martin stood up, winked and began to walk towards him. William held a finger up and attempted a casual stroll, slapping his arm on Martin's back and leading him out of earshot from the rest of the crowd.

'What. *The*. Fuck. Are you doing here?' he spat through gritted teeth.

'Making good on our little arrangement, old chap.' Martin dipped his hand into a nearby bowl of olives and popped one into his mouth, smacking his lips loudly as William looked at him in horror.

'This is my son's birthday party. You can't just—'

'Now, now, Billy boy. I can. And I have. So, let's say we work something out to avoid another unhappy reunion, shall we?'

William cleared his throat and gestured for Martin to follow him indoors and past the crowd. He unlocked a door in the hallway that opened into an airy home office, complete with antique furniture and large sash windows dressed with expensive-looking shutters.

'All right, what do you want? More money? What?'

'We want the flat, Billy.'

'Don't call me that. My name is – what do you mean you want the flat?'

Martin brought down his chin and raised an eyebrow, still snacking on the olives. He sucked the brine from his fore-finger and let out a satisfied sigh, wiping his wet digits on the arm of the expensive armchair he'd perched himself on. William grunted in disgust.

'We want you to gift it to the girls. Make them the owners and leave them alone for good.'

William began to laugh.

'You're asking me to give away, in effect, hundreds of thousands of pounds. To two whores?'

Martin leaped to his feet and pushed William against the door and its hefty handle, holding him in place with his elbow against his windpipe. William tried to speak but spluttered instead.

'P-please. Not here. *Please.*'

Martin looked into the man's desperate eyes and wanted to push harder. He wondered whether he had it in him to kill him. A knock at the door stopped him from considering it further.

'Will, darling. Are you in there? The entertainer's here,' said a woman's voice on the other side. William mouthed 'shit' and drew his hands together in prayer. Martin pointed a finger in his face and warned him not to say too much.

'Y-yes, I'm just on an important call. Two ticks!'

The pair made out a faint 'We fucking talked about this' on the other side as his wife's heavy footsteps decreased in volume in the direction of the door into the living room. Martin stood back to let the man breathe.

'All right. Fine. Take it. I'll have my solicitor draw up the deed and contact Land Registry, okay?'

'By when?'

'These things don't just take five minutes, you know. A month? Two? I'll have my solicitor liaise with you and Shirley and . . . and Lisa. Just please, leave me out of this. Do not come back here.' Martin shook the man's hand and winked again.

'All right, Bill. But if we don't hear anything for a week, consider those photos sent to every newspaper in the country, okay?' William nodded. Martin took the man's cheek in his right hand and gave it a hard squeeze, then left the room, briefly making eye contact with an exasperated-looking woman as he headed out the front door.

It took twelve weeks for the paperwork to be completed. Twelve weeks of the women still not quite feeling at ease in their own home. Jumping at unexpected rings on the buzzer. Heavy footsteps. Even spam calls from private numbers. William had been true to his word and had his solicitor call Shirley a week after Martin's visit. But there had always been a possibility that it wouldn't come off. William could have changed his mind, or used one of his high-profile contacts to issue a counter-threat. It never came. Instead, completion of the transfer arrived outside the flat one Monday evening via a thick envelope that would change their futures forever.

Shirley's daughter Megan came bursting through the door that evening with hair-raising energy, making Lisa and Judith jump. Both thought of the merits of being childless. The smile on Shirley's face seemed to scream the opposite. She came bounding in behind, fresh-faced and beaming at both of the women, who were lounging on the living room sofa together.

'I'm home, ladies!' Shirley shouted. The women looked at each other and rolled their eyes, wondering what had made her so chipper, though there needn't always be a reason with Shirley. She had a knack for exuding eagerness on the most mundane of days. Even in these trying circumstances.

'Jeeee-sus bloody Christ,' said Shirley as she walked up to Lisa and then Judith for a hug. 'I cannot wait for my bed.' Shirley met Judith's disapproving gaze. 'And sorry for using the Lord's name in vain, I know,' she said, flapping a large, partially ripped white envelope as if fanning herself. The two women squealed.

'Is that what I think it is?' said Lisa, ushering Shirley's child into her bedroom as Judith stood to attention.

'Have I got fucking news for you two,' Shirley said, drawing out quietly amused tuts from Judith. Shirley pulled the paper in a violent tug and ripped the envelope even more. It was over. It was finally over.

'Girls, I think this calls for a celebration,' she said, embracing the two women. In that moment, the trio felt closer than they had ever been.

Chapter Fifteen: The Shift

(Tottenham, 2008)

Lisa hadn't noticed how many clothes, accessories and pieces of furniture Judith had acquired since Delroy left. But seeing all of her possessions together, some waiting in meticulously organised suitcases for sending back home, challenged her judgement that her cousin hadn't ever embraced being here. She was everywhere: in the kitchen via the neatly stacked heavy-duty kitchen utensils and pots; in the almost overpowering smell of her favourite air freshener; in the general cleanliness of the place – especially now, before the party. Steam from the pressure cooker on the stove and the aroma of seasoning – curry powder, pimento, thyme – filled the air. They'd had space to spread their wings. There was fresh paint. Even the knick-knacks Delroy had littered the place with – old cricket trophies he'd taken with him from Jamaica; a big, dominating easychair in the living room; the film poster – had all gone. With the furniture pushed back for the shoobs, the flat looked almost sizeable.

She wondered how their respective groups would mingle. A larger part of her didn't care. Judith was far more supportive these days, in her own way. But she wasn't exactly happy about everything either. She still had questions about whether, now that Lisa and Shirley were homeowners, they'd keep 'selling themselves', a question even Lisa didn't know the answer to. Judith's lips still tightened and nose still wrinkled when Chioma dared give Lisa a peck on the cheek in her presence. Continued to look Lawrence up and down whenever he did anything she deemed unmanly. But there was a budding respect somewhere in there. She didn't feed information back to the family like Lisa's Auntie May had when Lisa had first moved to the UK. No longer pretended not to hear Chioma when she addressed her. Even complimented Lisa's hair – which she'd shaved off and dyed pink in the weeks following the attack. For that, at least, Lisa was thankful. Perhaps it was the bar she was measuring things against. When that bitch from school had run to her mother back home, saying she'd seen Lisa kissing a 'big 'oman' by the gully near church – a lie, but realistic enough given the suspicions that had swirled around her since her adolescence – it was enough for her to be sent away from everything she knew. To be regarded as disposable. Shameful. She'd lasted eight months in a crowded flat share before her colleague at one of her three jobs, Shirley, invited her to live with her in a flat she'd found with her boyfriend Delroy. It all felt like another life now.

As they prepared for their guests' arrival, she was glad that this, at least, they could share together without complications. That she could be who she was without hiding – it was her house now.

The Buck's Fizz Shirley had foisted on Judith had started to make her head feel fuzzy. She hadn't ever been much of a drinker. Alcoholic beverages were always too bitter, or sweet, or strong. She liked this tart concoction though. Chasing each sip with a glug of water helped even things out, the harsh snap of the bubbles reduced to ripples on her tongue. She had felt younger, getting ready with the girls earlier in the night, her sky-blue, knee-length, square-neckline dress hugged her body in ways that made Lisa and Shirley yelp the moment she stepped out of the bedroom in it.

'I didn't know you were hiding all that under there, Judith,' said Lisa, slapping her cousin's bottom and elbowing Shirley, who was egging her on, in the rib. She put on a matching cardigan to shut them up, but enjoyed the encouragement. It had been a while since she'd had a reason to dress up nice. Even if she was staying at home.

As the warmth from the drink coursed its way through Judith's body, she found herself marvelling at what they'd managed to create that night. It was 11 p.m. and the kitchen was already beginning to heave. There were guests from the restaurant: Clarke, from the kitchen at Cudjoe's, with his customary monologues about what he thought was causing the downfall of Black people that week. Betsy and Frank were there too, suffering through said speeches with groans and knowing glances. Some neighbours Shirley had invited, who clearly had come for the free food and drink alone, sitting in spare chairs in the living room, their full attention on the grease-stained paper plates that barely contained their meals or small white plastic cups full of rum punch with generously poured, nose-hair-burning levels of Wray & Nephew by their feet. There were Chioma and Lawrence, and several other loud friends of Lisa's that she hadn't met, all of them spirited and energetic, finger-pointing and cracking up every five minutes, some of their free-moving backsides threatening to topple the stacked, steaming plates to the floor; and Shirley's mad friends, none of whom, save for Martin, were white, who'd been getting on with Lisa's friends as if they'd known each other all their lives.

Mikey's arrival, though, was an unexpected bonus. Judith hadn't thought he'd show up. When she heard a husky voice utter her name from somewhere behind, her stomach fluttered. Still in the kitchen, empty plastic cup in hand, she turned around to check she'd heard correctly. It was him, all right. Dressed in slacks, a striped polo shirt and shoes that looked brand new, he sauntered towards the group from Cudjoe's with a lightness that she rarely saw in the restaurant. He was carrying a bottle of something brown, swinging it by his side as he embraced Clarke, Betsy and Frank one by one. By the time he got to Judith, he was beaming.

'You scrub up nice,' he said, handing her the drink, his eyes travelling down her body as he did so. Judith's usual blasé dismissal of such glances had been overtaken by a bout of shallow breath. She stuttered a little when she thanked him, irritated and confused at her lack of composure.

'Mi see you av' your good shoes on today,' she added, willing away her nerves and ushering in the more playful spirit she was used to when they spoke. He laughed and placed a hand on her shoulder, giving it a light squeeze. Judith wanted to say more, but he was beginning to float around and out of the room already, offering smiles and quips just as warm and cheeky to everyone around him. She'd never thought him a people person before; she'd only seen him around his employees and customers. The eager looks on the faces of everyone he spoke to disrupted that view. They all seemed to be glad to see him.

'Earth to Judith,' Shirley waved, as Judith snapped to.

'Weh yuh ah say?' she chuckled, shaking her head at her own distractedness. She hoped Shirley hadn't seen her staring. She'd never hear the end of it.

'You want a top-up?' So she hadn't noticed. Judith nodded without thinking and took the concoction from Shirley, thanking her. Shirley, it turned out, was a brilliant host. She hadn't stopped checking in on guests since the first one – an overeager neighbour with a strong taste for macaroni pie, escovitch fish and gossip about the other neighbours – arrived at 8 p.m. Judith felt something like admiration for her.

The groups were weaving in and out of rooms and circles with ease now, the music blaring out of the speakers in the living room with such force that the bass made it feel like the flat was shaking. Shirley's friend, DJ D, had himself up behind a trestle table, and was treating his duties like a real gig, his dark sunglasses and bobbing head giving him an air of stylish expertise. He'd drawn crowds through his various sets: some throwback reggae, dancehall and soca from the likes of Dennis Brown, Red Rat, Terror Fabulous, Beenie Man, Marlon Asher, Square One, Burning Flames, Bunji Garlin and more; a garage and grime set featuring artists like Kano, Skepta, More Fire Crew and Nasty Crew, DJ Luck & MC Neat, Wookie, So Solid, and a slew of hits like T-Pain's 'Buy U a Drank', Lil Wayne's 'A Milli', Crazy Cousinz's 'Bongo Jam', and T2's 'Heartbroken'. Clarke, by then, had moved onto the dancefloor, shuffling a little awkwardly through each set in a way that amused the younger guests. Frank, meanwhile, was making his way through several dance partners, treating each woman he wined with as if they were the last on the planet.

In the hum of kitchen chatter and blaring music, it felt nice for Judith to let herself go a little. She'd been talking to Lisa and Chioma and Mikey about Jamaica, romanticising the parts she'd found trying when she lived there: the bureaucracy, the community spirit, even the potholes. Mikey surprised her when he said he didn't miss much of it at all. He was happy enough with the odd holiday, but living there again would be a mistake. He was more interested in West African countries these days. Maybe Ghana. And would Chioma recommend Nigeria?

'Haven't been since I was eight. But you could try it and let me know if you want,' Chioma said, clinking cups with Mikey. It was a perspective that Lisa, who was happily drunk by now, understood. Not Judith. They debated the pros and cons with playful vigour, drawing in passers-by who, on the way to topping up their drinks, found the conversation riveting.

DJ D had returned to throwback dancehall, distracting Lisa from the conversation she had moments ago been incredibly invested in. The pulsating bassline of Lady Saw's 'Man Is the Least' forced her body upright.

'Look how she a gwan,' Mikey said, laughing. 'Go on, go and dance.'

Lisa yanked her girlfriend's and cousin's arms in the direction of the kitchen door and ushered them towards the living room. Shirley had, with her friends and a bouncing Martin, already taken to the middle of the room. The three housemates found their way towards each other and began to belt their renditions of the chorus to the ceiling, Judith's familiarity with the tune surprising the two younger women.

The track, which, really, was about the artist's disdain for women who waste time arguing over men, felt like a mantra to the women. A reminder of the banes of their lives up until recently and the catharsis of being free of them. Really free. The set began to move into more frenzied territory; Judith patted the women on the back and made again for the kitchen. A sense of calm washed over her as she walked away from them and towards the spot she'd claimed as her base.

The kitchen had thinned out a bit since earlier. The music was the focus now. With the alcohol running lower and the once-full aluminium trays now dwindling to scraps, it was a room dedicated to respite.

'My girl, you've thrown a proper good party,' said Frank, who was gnawing on a fleshless chicken wing. Judith sighed and smiled as she let herself rock back against the kitchen countertop.

'Tired?'

Judith nodded yes. It was around 1 a.m., and the gravity of the task of cleaning once everyone had left was not lost on her. She moved to the kitchen table and fixed herself her first plate of the night – a hidden portion of curry goat, rice and peas, salad and coleslaw she'd set aside for herself earlier. Frank wagged a knowing finger at her, impressed with her forward thinking. He joined her at the table.

'Judith, if I tell you something, will you keep it a secret?' he said with the mischievousness of a five-year-old, the sharp tinge of alcohol on his breath. Judith raised her eyebrow at him. Satisfied with her reaction, he continued.

'I think Mikey has a thing for you, you know.'

'Chupid,' she said, smiling more than she'd meant to. Frank leaned in closer, his teeth a neat, exposed row of white.

'Nah, I'm serious. He won't stop talking about you. Hasn't stopped since you started working at the restaurant.'

Judith kissed her teeth, but she was still smirking.

'Yuh too fool-fool,' she said, pushing at his chest and shaking her head.

'You wouldn't go out with him?'

'Frank.'

'But—'

'Frank.'

'All right, all right. Just think about it. Mi tink seh there's something there. Speak of the devil.'

Judith looked up to see Mikey with his arms folded by the doorway, looking down at the floor. She wondered how long he'd been there. He looked hurt. Or bored. Frank, oblivious, called after him. He grunted and briefly approached them, before making his excuses about having to leave.

'Going so soon?' Judith said, trying to ignore Frank's widening eyes, hoping she could change the subject and put those silly playground matchmaking efforts to rest. Mikey shrugged without meeting her gaze and said something about having to drive Clarke home, 'cah him too drunk'. Frank pushed his lips upwards and nodded his head in Mikey's direction, a too blatant signal to Judith that he suspected Mikey was in one of his moods again. Mikey caught Frank's gesture, narrowed his eyes and whipped his body around to face the door, ignoring calls from Frank to relax. Sighing, he continued towards the opening of the kitchen and walked straight out of it. The sound of the front door slamming followed him seconds later. Judith didn't understand what had happened. Frank, distracted by one of the women who'd come into the room, oblivious to the awkward situation before her, didn't seem to care. It may well have been 'one of his moods', Judith told herself. It wouldn't be the first time. If it had been, though, she suspected she'd feel a lot less crushed. She distracted herself with clearing plates.

Chapter Sixteen: The Class

(East London, 2010)

Judith had been at the top of her class all her life. It was an achievement she wore with quiet pride, her heart soaring with every A grade she collected. She worked hard and knew she deserved to be recognised for it. In Jamaica as a child, her know-it-all tendencies had rubbed classmates up the wrong way. She would show other students up when teachers singled them out, answering questions they'd been stumped by, causing them to get the cane. In one incident, her crush, Garnet – back then, a naughty boy with eyes so bright and teeth so straight that everyone called him 'Sweet' – got it. Sitting in her classroom at college, she remembered how, back in high school, he bore his eyes into her while the teacher was slapping his hand with a ruler, his eyes narrowing with each thwack, she'd almost wanted to turn bad there and then. Almost. It took as little as witnessing him walk into a door later that day, nearly choking on his gum, to change her mind.

In the years since, Judith realised that the feeling of soaring above the crowd made her feel better than apologising for being smart. She didn't think herself better than everyone. She just knew she was capable. In the stillness of her new classrooms in a run-down east London college, she kept those early lessons, and the weight of her family's wellbeing, in her mind and firmly on her shoulders.

'If you'll turn to page twenty-five, you'll see how these exam questions are often worded,' her stocky, blonde-haired teacher said dryly to the disengaged room. Her voice could make anyone sleepy. She would've joined in on the jokes with her classmates if she had the confidence. Or if she hadn't been gripped by the fear of falling behind. There was too much at stake for silliness. This had to work.

Save for four men from West African countries, most of the people on her course were women, none from the UK. They were white, Black, South American and South Asian. Nigerian, Ecuadorian, Brazilian, Polish, Kosovan, Somali, Iranian, Ugandan, Ghanaian, Indian. Some bonded over shared languages or words, others through the late lunches or dinners they brought in, or common interests. They'd gossip about the soaps they'd seen the night before, or sports games foreign to her. Judith didn't share much. She liked church, reading her bible, keeping order. She enjoyed cooking. She had fun at her job. She loved her family, would do anything for them. But idle chit-chat? Judith told herself she liked it at first, she was there to learn, not make friends. But she'd garnered a stand-offish reputation, and she noticed some hostility from the others – especially when she cut them off to answer correctly in class.

One evening, half an hour before her class was due to start, Judith sat down in the small space allotted to students for breaks. The furniture – yellow foam poking out of cracked faux leather seats, unsteady tables – wobbled at the slightest contact. Judith always got to class at least half an hour early. She used the time to study or read magazines. It cleared her mind. She was here to train herself into a better position in society. To get her qualification and save herself from long commutes and gruelling shifts at work. She could send more money back home to her mother and siblings then, instead of the clothes and change she scrimped to send back every few months.

Judith brought a plastic container of leftover oxtail, white rice and plantain, with her to class. She was glad no one was there yet, so she could enjoy sucking on the bone in peace. The white students looked at her strangely when she did that. As if sensing her comfort, a group of her peers arrived and sat themselves on the table opposite her, laughing together as they sat down. Judith felt awkward. It had been a couple of days since she'd bumped into one of them on the tube, pretending not to see when they smiled and waved a few feet away from her – a last ditch attempt to crack the nut. At class later that day, she had retreated further into herself, hostility masking discomfort.

'Is this seat taken?' the brown-skinned Brazilian student, who'd come up behind her, said, sitting down before she answered. Judith shook her head and wiped her mouth, though there was nothing on it. She'd never been a messy eater. 'Judith, right?' the student said. She was a kind-looking woman, no older than forty, with short, greying, fluffy black hair and a pear-shaped frame. They'd never spoken in all the months of this course. She seemed nice enough. Judith flashed a pained smile at the woman and swiftly went back to her food.

'I'm Clara,' she said with an outstretched hand, setting down a steaming container of what looked like a black bean stew, plantain, greens and a dark meat of some kind. They carried on eating in silence, the other table stealing glances at them.

'Yuh food look nice,' Judith whispered eventually.

'Sorry?' the woman replied, not quite hearing her.

'It look nice. Smell good too.'

'Thank you. It's feijoada,' she added, tipping her container in Judith's direction. 'So um, pig, black bean, greens, rice, farofa,' she said, trying to think of the English word for the cassava flour she'd sprinkled on top of her meal.

'Far-wah? Ah wah dat?' Judith said involuntarily, clamping her mouth in shock at her own curtness.

Clara laughed. 'Cassava? I think is what you call it? Do you know it?'

'Yes, yes, mi know cassava,' Judith added.

'We have –' she pointed at the yellow powder sitting on the brown stew beneath '– ca-ss-a-v-a in my country too.' Judith felt herself cringe as she resorted to a patronising pace of English and corrected herself.

'Yuh 'av *oxtail* inna Brazil? That's what mi ah eat . . . that's what I'm eating.'

Clara sensed Judith was trying.

'Yes, we have it,' she added. 'Rabada. It's so tasty. I'll bring some one day.'

'Yuh wan try mine?'

Clara's eyes lit up. 'Yes, yes! You have some of mine too.'

The women took turns transferring small portions of their dishes into each other's containers, both of them commenting on the plantain they both had, not knowing what else to say. They ate on in silence, exchanging grins and hums of gratitude for ten minutes before class. Though Judith knew they wouldn't go on to be friends, she was grateful for the effort Clara had put in, and for the chance to make one too.

Chapter Seventeen:
The Discovery

(Elephant and Castle, 2010)

When Frank woke up bleary-eyed and horny that morning, he thought he had a good idea of how his day would go. The sun had woken him from his heavy sleep hours ago, but he still hadn't found the energy to move. It always went that way when he'd accidentally fallen asleep in a strange woman's bed. This time, he already regretted staying over. It was coming up to 10 a.m., and they'd each been tossing and turning in that more-awake-than-you-want-to-let-on way people do when testing the waters with people they don't quite know. He didn't want her to mistake it for shyness. He'd just never worked out how to leave immediately, like some men could. Frank was more caresser than bang and dash. A romantic at heart with a people-pleasing problem, he'd often say what he felt women, friends, family – himself – wanted to hear, thinking it a balm for the disappointment that would inevitably follow when he let them down. He was yearning for something real, even if it was fleeting. He mastered it each time.

The twenty-year-old lying beside Frank wouldn't be the last to be on the receiving end of that hopeful, naive charm. But he would make her feel like she was. He turned to face her, stroking the elastic around the edge of her bonnet, his lips curled slightly into a grin he'd long been told melted hearts, dampened panties.

'Morning,' he whispered, his smile now infectious. She whispered it back, sensually, with a performative tinge of raspiness that gave away a little too much eagerness. He could tell she wanted him to stick around a little while longer. To continue the charade of coupledom he'd initiated the night before. Cooking for her. Telling her he'd never met anyone like her. Even opening up about his upbringing, an impulse at this point that always made him shudder the next day. There was something about the warm embrace of a woman, the pillowy warmth of a bare breast, that awakened haunting memories of all that could have been, all that he felt he'd squandered since he'd arrived in London as a teenager. He grimaced as images from his monologue the night before entered his mind. How soothed he'd allowed himself to be by the naive reassurances the girl had offered, by the manufactured intimacy he'd engineered that now overwhelmed him with shame. He glanced upward and saw her eyes searching his for a sign that it meant something too. He didn't need this, not now.

'Mmm,' he murmured in a gravelly tone, tracing his fingers along her buttery brown skin. 'You tired me out last night, girl.'

'*Me?* What about you?' she said back in a way he'd heard many times before. Ignoring it, he snaked his fingers across her belly, inching closer to the puffy, prickly skin above her vulva. He whispered words of flattery into her ear. She lapped it up. He moved his hand down further, between her lips. She moaned loudly. Continuing, he pushed his fingers deep inside her with a little difficulty. After a few minutes, her moans had turned into theatrical panting, her body twisting with what he wondered might be performative pleasure. Had she come? He hadn't the desire to find out either way. He retreated, kissing her on the forehead before swinging his legs out to stand up.

'You're leaving?' the girl asked. The look on her face pained him a little. Her expressions oscillated between disappointment and feigned indifference. He turned his back to her and began to pull his clothes over himself with care, words escaping him. He didn't make eye contact with her until he reached the corridor of the small new-build flat, where the faint sound of chatter from her student housemates broke the silence. Standing on her doorstep, he took her hands in his and kissed them gently as she sighed.

'I'll call you later, yeah?' Frank said, lying as he gazed into the girl's hazel eyes.

'Is it,' she said in a deadpan tone, perhaps onto his game. Not wishing to confirm either way, he turned and walked with purpose away from her and filled his mind with thoughts of anything else.

Frank always struggled with this part. How easily it came to him to begin these short-lived affairs, and how hard he found it to transition out of them. He wondered sometimes if his charm was, in fact, a curse. If his effortless engagement with people was, in fact, not the gift his friends would often praise it as. Were it such a blessing, he wouldn't have left a trail of children and disgruntled mothers in his wake. His heart wouldn't sink to the bottom of his chest each time an unsaved number flashed across his phone screen, making the prospect of finding out that another woman he'd bedded was late and keeping the baby a likely possibility. If only he could bring himself to have a vasectomy. Charmaine and Shelly, his eldest daughters, the only two he'd planned, had planted that seed in his mind a few years before, with the arrival of his youngest child, Dylan, whose mother had moved back to Sweden to give birth, and hadn't been seen, or pursued him since.

'You really want to spend your life leaving kids all over the gaffe, Daddy?' Charmaine had asked when he produced the sonogram of their sixth new sibling, hoping to soften them. He always wondered if this, along with minor brushes with the law, had been the 'trouble' his mother had warned about when he'd first touched soil in England, after spending the first fourteen years of his life in Jamaica. How she looked at him when he acted out. He was bewildered by his new life in London, the easy curriculum that bored him and raised his teachers' suspicions that he was cheating. The general assumption from others that he was stupid when he stopped trying. He began bunking off after about a year of trying and failing to prove himself in class, both intellectually and socially, a combination that led to detentions and unwarranted scoldings from irate teachers. To them, he was a pest. But to the girls, to the guys, he was admired.

In Jamaica, Frank had been a model student. It wasn't until his mother's departure for the UK, when he was ten, that the malaise set in. His step-grandmother, a strict, proud, paranoid woman with other grandchildren to attend to and little patience for him, seemed exhausted by his presence. She'd never liked his mother, and he paid the price in beatings, snide comments and general neglect when his grandfather's back was turned. He missed his mother terribly during those years. Wanted to call her every day. Felt abandoned, comforted only by the goods she'd send home for the family, and him, in large steel barrels. Sometimes, when no one was around, he'd bring the clothes she sent to his nostrils, hoping to catch a whiff of her perfume, or the talcum powder she dutifully applied to her chest. It never came.

Being the second-born son meant staying behind with his step-grandmother until his family on the other side of the world was ready for him. He understood why his mother, and then, six months later, his older brother, had left him for what felt like for ever. They were providing for everyone. Working hard. Doing what, he assumed on their departure, they felt he couldn't. He longed to be older. Stronger. To prove himself. But all signs on his arrival suggested he was incapable. He channelled those feelings of abandonment and ineptitude into late nights, cars and girls. The mornings after were almost always followed by harsh words and a slipper to the back of the leg. Where had he been? With who? And why did he have to drive so damn fast?

The scoldings rang through his mind as he made his way to Charmaine's in his car. For all his failings in life, when he was with his eldest he felt like the best version of a father he could have hoped to be. She was forgiving in a way that his other children weren't. Brutally honest in ways Shelly, his second child, often struggled to be. He respected Charmaine for her fearlessness. For her pragmatism. Her strengths as a mother to two small children. Frank shook his head and lightly tapped the steering wheel, trying to shake the tellings off, the cold shiver that ran through his body when his mother was vex, away. They haunted him not because he couldn't take the criticism, but because he knew better. He always had. The problem was that the guilt was a gateway to those very mistakes, an easing of the sneaking suspicion he'd always had about himself that he was – as he believed his step-grandmother, mother, teachers thought – fundamentally 'bad'.

His mother's voice had sounded an alarm in his subconscious the very moment he'd first been caught and fined for driving without a licence. Working himself sick, getting drunk and going out were the only things that helped to drown it out. He sought comfort in the form of a pair of big tits, or a bountiful backside, despite Gina, his long-term partner and mother to his first two children, waiting worried at home for him. When he was eventually disqualified from driving after being caught without insurance, the sound of his mother was almost unbearable. When he received his first prison sentence, leaving a few more children and partners in his wake, the sound was deafening. He was a piece of shit. Might as well roll around in it.

Frank would often call himself 'chupid' and 'useless' under his breath, comforted by the idea of receiving his just punishment from the person he respected most, even if she hadn't actually uttered the words. She'd given up on that a long time ago, and her fatigue was hard to stomach. She was withdrawn and forlorn. She offered up sighs more often than words. Closed her eyes and leaned her head back for ten seconds at a time when the news was especially bad. Mostly, she just worried about him. Silently. Obsessively. Sometimes he wondered if the cacophony of that silence would kill him one day. Or drive him to do it himself. Sitting outside of Charmaine's flat in Harlesden, where she was cooking Sunday dinner, his anxiety eased slightly. In her house, in her presence, it was one of few places he felt at home.

'You lot don't know what you're missing out on. Salad cream with curry goat is elite.' The small living room, filled with six of Charmaine's siblings, her husband John, Frank and her two small twin boys, erupted into a blend of groans and laughter. She continued her defence.

'Listen, yeah, you lot nyam up the coleslaw I make every month no matter what mi ah cook. That nuh have salad cream in it?'

'It's not the same, girl,' said Angela, her gangly-limbed sixteen-year-old sister, garnering mutters of agreement and a shoulder shake from John.

'Tell ar!' John added, laughing as he wrangled their squirming toddlers on the black leather sofa on the other end of the room.

Charmaine's father winked at her and offered his support. He was always on her side. She lapped it up, glad to have someone to encourage her. Glad to have him around.

'And just for that, Daddy's the only one I'm fixing a plate for. The rest of you are on your own.'

Charmaine's Sunday dinners were always like this. If it wasn't odd condiment pairings they'd get onto her for, it was her love of brash costume jewellery, or bejewelled high-heel boots.

'You all right, Pat Butcher?' her sister Shelly would often jibe, to roaring laughter. No matter how many times they heard the joke, her familial audience would without fail react as if it were the first time.

It had been about a decade of this. Ten years since the surprise birth of her little sister, Tash, a child wise beyond her years who felt like a daughter to her these days. Ten years since her father had assured the rest of them that this would be the last time he'd break their hearts the way he had. Ten years since she'd called a family meeting, to sort through years of neglected issues between her, Shelly, Frank and the rest of the siblings she'd missed out on getting to know for all this time.

She remembered that day as if it were still unfolding before her. The boho skirt, concho belt and black vest top that hugged the curves of her body. The icy coolness and sickly-sweet scent of the hair gel and Blue Magic grease she'd used to slick back her short, relaxed ponytail. How heavily it had rained despite the time of year, the stench of petrichor filling the humid air that blew gently through the cracked windows in the living room where they had gathered like sardines in her mother's house. The anguished yet proud look on her father's face as she took the lead with breaking the ice, while he rocked his new baby girl, her new baby sister. How her aching heart settled momentarily at the sight of Tash's wrinkled little face and compact, wriggling body. How it felt as if it would burst the moment she held her tiny torso against her chest.

Charmaine was in her early twenties then, and, despite having an amicable, respectful relationship with her father, had always been painfully aware of how much had to go unsaid to keep things light. It was a charade that ate at her in ways that her sister Shelly never seemed to struggle with; silence and deflection had always been her default, just like their father. As Charmaine looked around the room, she felt glad she hadn't inherited those traits. They'd never have made it this far as a family otherwise. A smile crept over her face, momentarily deepening the faint lines that age had begun to imprint at the sides of her eyes and mouth over the past couple of years. She caught her husband's eye and blew him a kiss, taking in his warmth from across the room. He was nothing like Frank. Nothing like anyone in her family. Charmaine's family would tower over others in most rooms they walked into. He would take up horizontal space. They would fight to be heard. He would take others in, encouraging them, just like he was now, with his small, dark-brown eyes, settling their spirit with his quiet, sensible confidence. Meeting him at work seven years earlier, where she'd managed the office and he'd managed the company accounts, was extraordinary in how unremarkable it was. Thrilling even. She'd never stopped being thankful for that security.

By the early evening, the happy, full-bellied guests had already begun to succumb to short-lived slumber in the living room. John and Frank had cleared the plates and were busying themselves with the washing-up in the kitchen, where Charmaine and Shelly sat at a small fold-out table, smoking and complaining about the soaring food prices.

'I went down to the butcher the other day. Guess how much it cost me? Six, almost seven pound for a kilo of meat we're paying now,' said Charmaine between puffs.

'Fifty p for a likkle chocolate bar. Don't even get me started on toilet roll,' Shelly chimed in, flicking ash into the ceramic dish on the table. John, now drying the dishes, nodded in agreement.

'Them dyam teefs,' Frank exclaimed as he vigorously scrubbed the weighty Dutch pot the curry had been resting in. 'Them run the country into the ground, and then turn around and say –' he steadied himself, cocking his head to the side as he put on his best English geezer accent and raised his palm to his chest in faux outrage '– "Ooh, immigration is too high. The bloody foreigners are taking our jobs."'

'Yeah, jobs they're too lazy to do themselves,' added Shelly, kissing her teeth.

'Tell them again, Shelly,' Frank added, slapping a dish cloth against his thigh.

'Honestly, I think we'd be better off going back home,' Charmaine added.

'Kakafawt!' spluttered Frank.

'No, Daddy, I honestly think—'

'Ee-hee. I bet you do,' Frank replied with a tinge of sarcasm that Charmaine met by raising her hands in mock defeat.

It always went this way when talk of leaving the country came up. For all his frustrations with 'this place', as he often referred to it, living here still had a hold on her father that Charmaine could never quite understand. She'd seen what it had done to him. How tired it had made him to travel up and down the city, working cash-in-hand on decorating and carpentry jobs that sent sharp pains through his limbs and paid him much less than he deserved. She'd never lived in Jamaica, but the ease she felt there, the sense of belonging, had always felt like a much more worthy trade. And besides, her father hadn't lived there since he was a kid. The country had surely changed for the better since then. The cracked, uneven roads certainly had, even if only marginally.

'Mi nah lie, this country will test your patience. But it nuh worth leaving over. Not even with costs going up.'

'He thinks he's too good for back a yard now, innit, Shelly?' The sisters tittered, knowing he'd take the bait.

'Yuh ever been a Jamaican hospital?' Frank added, surprising no one with his go-to defence.

'No, Daddy,' the daughters said in unison, rolling their eyes behind his back while John, never one to get in the middle, ignored them all.

'Yuh ever haffi send yuh pickney fi walk two mile pon foot fi go school?'

'No, Daddy.'

'He hasn't either,' whispered Charmaine, making her sister giggle and their father's nostrils flare. He kissed his teeth as Shelly placed a hand on his shoulder, trying to calm him as he began to stutter.

'Yuh-yuh wan yuh pickney dem fi get beats at school?'

'Might be good for 'em, you never know,' Shelly added in jest.

'The Jamaica you see when unu go pon holiday is not the same as living it, day in day out. Yuh see how mi granny poor. How yuh family back home poor. How your cousin dem harass yuh for "a likkle change" when mi tek you fi di first time. Yuh forget?'

Charmaine and Shelly looked at the floor, their hanging heads a sign of defeat.

'Yeah, yeah. Yuh chat too much. Englan' nah perfect. It's not. But it's a better life.'

'Yeah, for some,' said Charmaine, avoiding the paper napkin her father lobbed lightly at her.

'Yuh nuh know weh yuh ah chat bout,' Frank added under his breath, his eyes downcast in a manner that filled the room with tension. His heart felt heavier with each passing glance between his daughters. Desperate to lighten the load, he plastered a grin on his face, torn between the brutal knowledge of a world he knew and a fantasy they'd dipped in and out of during two- and four-week visits interspersed with hotel stays and expensive dining. He didn't blame them, really. He'd trade his life in London for their version of Jamaica too if he could.

Chapter Eighteen: The Unveiling

(Harlesden, 2011)

It was coming up to 1 p.m. when Frank pulled up outside the restaurant. He'd come to do some last-minute painting for Mikey. It was a mysterious request. Frank guessed what it was about, and was intrigued. Mikey had been pottering about in the basement after hours for years now, organising papers that he let no one see or touch. The week before, he'd ordered fifteen photo frames of varying sizes and styles, leaving them stacked on top of their box in a messy heap one evening, explaining nothing.

Frank had ignored Mikey's exaggerated cautions in the past – the dangers of using certain cleaning products on his old café furniture, strange requests to lock the toilets in bad weather, because he could hear the cubicle doors flapping in the wind (he insisted on keeping the bathroom window open). He had discovered over the years that defying those rules somehow gained him Mikey's respect.

Mikey wasn't there when he entered. He was often late, arriving 'just in time', according to himself. Frank seized the moment, heading for the basement and that box. He felt like a child sneaking a sweetie from the kitchen in the middle of the night.

He took his time peeling back the flimsy, worn piece of tape that held the box closed. He didn't want it to tear, lest Mikey discover. The flaps sprang up from the volume of whatever was inside. Peering in, he could see photos. Beautiful photos that made his heart stop the minute he locked eyes with one of the subjects. He flicked through the first four, marked FOR DISPLAY in red permanent marker, holding up the most impressive ones to the light, searching for clues: a date, a note, a location. So here it was. Mikey's art. It's real! He picked up a handful of smaller prints and flicked through them like a flip book. There were photos in colour and in black and white, some of protests, others of people rejoicing. Some perfect illustrations of the memories Frank had of London as a young man, Black and brown people rejoicing, in mourning, flirting, resisting. A Black man wearing sunglasses standing with his hands on his hips in Westbourne Park tube station; a round Black woman lost in music as she strikes the snare drum of the drum kit before her, with a caption reading 'Big Linda'. *Must have been famous back in the day*, he figured. Then, dressed in a sports tracksuit, leaning forward, left hand under his chin, right hand balled up into a fist as he looked off to the side: it was Sugar Ray Robinson.

Could it be a postcard? Frank wondered, searching for clues that it was a copy. He couldn't find anything, only Mikey's illegible scribbles and signature at the back. Frank flicked through the rest, pulling out the ones with the recognisable faces, or unrecognisable backdrops – some seemingly taken in Europe. Maybe Italy?

'Bumbaaa,' Frank whispered repeatedly. This must be what Mikey wanted him to work on that day. He picked out the photos that struck him the most, sorting through the frames for the right size. Mikey was at least ready to move forward. Good on him. Frank put the photos back to resume the painting job upstairs.

By the time he'd mixed the paint, Mikey burst through the door, panting and irritable. He swore at the door for being too heavy. Threw off his hat and exhaled loudly.

'You know, too many of these likkle yout dem just run out into the road without looking these days. Just shoot straight out, listening to them music, inviting cars to lick dem down.'

Frank grunted agreement and continued to mix his paint.

'And one of them! You should have seen wah him wear. Looked like it was 1985 again, mi tell yuh.'

Mikey hadn't looked at Frank. Too busy moving around, moaning. When he looked up, any frustrations he was feeling transferred.

'Eh, Frank,' he said in a voice that caused the skin on Frank's cheeks to tighten.

'Jesus, wah mi done now,' he muttered, regretting it, in case Mikey heard him. He hadn't.

'Why are you mixing paint? A who tell yuh fi do that?' Mikey said, clearly forgetting those were the exact instructions he'd given. Frank knew better than to protest. Scraping the excess mint-green paint off the mixer, he set it to the side on the roller tray, waiting for further scolding.

'Pay attention, bwoi! Yuh wan get paint all over the shop?'

Frank didn't have the energy to tell him, even if he had asked him to put up the photos – which he hadn't – that doing it before a paint job made absolutely no sense. Mikey was in a mood to argue.

'Yes. Nuh budda worry about the paint. Leff it. Photos first but covered, yeah? Here, take this.'

Mikey handed Frank some sheets of black tissue paper and masking tape. So he wanted a reveal, Frank thought, following the instructions in silence and beginning to cover the frames up. He was staying out of the way.

'Eh-eh, why you look so miserable?' said Mikey. He did that sometimes: played clueless when owning his mistakes would have worked better. He'd agonise over errors, worrying he'd upset Frank, or whoever got caught in the crossfire between his ego and his anxieties. But he'd never say. To Frank, it was no bother. When he cared about a person, he wrote off tantrums as mere character flaws, tiny in comparison to the beauty they exuded.

'Just tell me where you want them, Mikey,' said Frank, who'd scaled a ladder next to a seating booth.

'Over there suh,' Mikey replied, pointing with his lips, an instruction as clear to Frank as a baby's coo to its parent. It went on that way for a while. Frank would suggest hanging spots with the tip of his finger, get the silent go ahead from Mikey and hammer into the wall, placing the covered frames just so, until black rectangles covered the room. Mikey helped Frank off the ladder. Frank smiled and patted Mikey on the shoulder.

'Happy?'

Mikey took a few steps back and stopped to look up at the frames, judging their placement like a curator. He was terrified. He was elated. The feverish beginnings of his dream beginning to play out before his eyes.

'Yes, yes. I think so.'

Frank moved towards the old man, who seemed paralysed on the spot, and rested his palm on his shoulder before giving it a gentle squeeze. Mikey hesitated for a second and then placed his hand on top of Frank's, lightly sighing as he did so.

'You should be proud, Mikey. You really should,' said Frank without moving his hand, stopping himself before he gave himself away.

'Keep it between us for now,' Mikey said, moving away a couple of steps to get a different angle of the room.

'If the customers ask questions?'

'Tell them Cudjoe's gone mad,' Mikey answered plainly.

Was he going to do this all over again? Mikey thought to himself. What if no one cared? What if these walls were as far as his life's work would go? He looked around the room as if to check, half expecting to be flooded with doubt. All he saw was the flawed good. On its last legs, sure. But look at the community it served. Think of the laughter and satisfaction that this place ran on. Did he want to do this?

Mikey clapped his hands together once more, answering his own question.

It was a cooler evening than usual. But you wouldn't have known it in Cudjoe's on the night of the dinner. The heating was turned up to the max, as per. Mikey's guests were hit with a wall of warmth as they entered, washing over them with the heat of a thousand suns, pressing them to abandon heavy coats and woollen hats as if they were alight. It was an expense staff members had told Mikey to cut back on over the years. 'We back home?' newer punters would joke, melting. He'd ignore them, dismissing the suggestions for energy-efficient practice as 'bloody rubbish'. His parents prepared food with pearls of sweat dampening their hair and faces. What was the problem?

The first guests arrived. In a frantic bout of calls one evening, Mikey had spoken to them one by one, a firm tone impressing upon his guests that the invitation was non-negotiable. The private viewing element of the evening would be a surprise. He'd invited them to look at photos. The rest, spanning several decades, would be for sorting later. Maybe an art collector. Some of those rolls of film might be worth heaps of money. He would move one step at a time. He started by asking the six members of the Cudjoe's family to join him: Ivy, his head waiter; his chefs Betsy, Inez and Clarke plus Judith and Frank. 'Family' in the least sentimental sense. They had become permanent fixtures in his life, but they were not 'friends'. In they came between six and seven that evening, one by one, ready to swelter quietly if it meant being treated to a nice night in.

Inez and Clarke arrived first. Though they'd worked there for years, their rapport was as frosty as day one. Inez had worked for Mikey the longest, and liked to remind people when she felt the need. Clarke's arrival, two years later, had been a moment for the spiel. 'Ah ME seh make this kitchen what it is, y'ear?' she'd protest, banging her wooden spoon on the counter top whenever she believed Clarke was interfering, which was relatively often. He wasn't to touch her good spoon, or turn down the heat when her stews and curries were on the verge of burning.

Clarke was quiet, matter of fact and pushing forty; Inez was louder, and, though she didn't look it, slowly cruising towards her eighties. The gulf between them grew wider by the month. They tried to avoid the snares of a mother–son dynamic, but it took hold from the moment Clarke, on his first day, questioned why her ackee and saltfish was swimming in oil.

'Yuh wan serve ackee and saltfish with that grease?' he asked while Mikey slapped him on the back of the neck, appreciating his cheek. Inez quietly took off her apron, folded it up, and shuffled out of the room. Things calmed down over the years, disdain for each other reduced to a spark rather than a full-blown blaze. They found a way to co-exist: Inez would ignore him, her silent demands for respect emanating through her pursed lips, elongated neck and lack of eye contact. Clarke played innocent, only joking at her expense when confident it would go over her head, or only irritate her marginally. Betsy, always late, held the trio together. At twenty-five, she was doted on by both elders. She'd been raised in London but had sharpened her cooking skills in Jamaica during a three-year stint, punishment for falling in with the wrong crowd and skiving off school as a teen. When she came back, she was as focused and driven as her parents had wanted her to be; except that they'd lost her trust – and a bit of her light – in the process.

'Greetings to the gruesome twosome,' Mikey shouted as the pair awkwardly made their way through the door.

'Move nuh man!' shouted Inez, as she shimmied her round body into the room, causing Clarke, lanky and awkward, to stumble back slightly. Mikey loved the theatrics but pretended to pay no attention, waving them over to the area he'd set up in the middle of the restaurant.

'Where did you get that tablecloth?' said Clarke, still

confused by Mikey's effort. The tablecloth, a thick cream sheet that felt like silk, but probably wasn't, had been draped over one of the larger tables, obscuring the vibrant red underneath. Mikey had placed a silver candelabra in the centre, with tealights dotted around. There were proper place settings with salad, entrée and dessert utensils. Napkins replaced the paper tissues in the metal dispensers. There were red chairs, usually in the basement. Under the romantic lighting, they looked antique. Perhaps they'd always been. Though you'd barely notice them under the warm glow of the candlelit room, on the walls, in between the existing prints and photographs, sat six new frames, covered with thin black crepe paper.

'Yuh done inspecting, Clarky?' said Mikey, watching them circle the table.

Clarke smiled, replied 'Yeah man,' without returning his gaze and sat on the bar stool opposite. Maybe Mikey needed something, he thought. Perhaps he was dying. Clarke inspected the old man's eyes for signs of fatigue. They looked the same as always – small, brown, watery and vibrant.

Mikey gestured towards the table and told Clarke to sit in his proper place, while Inez, who'd seen the place cards, sat in the right spot with her head cocked up at an angle, the teacher's pet.

'Thanks, Mikey, now I can look pon Inez pretty face all night long,' said Clarke, taking his seat opposite her, suspicious that the seating arrangement had been some kind of jibe.

'Rude likkle . . .' Inez mumbled back.

'Miss Inez, is everything okay?' Mikey offered, half joking.

She'd replaced her headtie and hairnet with her fanciest wig –
a curly, neatly cropped bob – and her favourite floral dress.
She looked nice. But Mikey wasn't disrupting the jokes with
sentimentality. Keep it light.

The rest arrived together ten minutes later. Frank ignored
the place card and took a seat next to Clarke. Mikey, a little
annoyed, sat at the opposite end, trying his best not to glare
at Frank for his impertinence, as Judith made her way next to
Mikey. Betsy, who'd busied herself with opening and sharing
out the bottle of white wine on the table, eventually took a
break from helping and sat in front of Judith on the other side.

'So . . .' Judith began, not sure of what she was going to say.
'To what do we owe the occasion?'

Mikey wagged a finger that said 'not so fast', the forced
sense of mystery he'd created beginning to overwhelm him.

'First, we eat. Then we talk.'

A kissing of the teeth from one of them interrupted
his flow.

'So we must just . . . sit in silence and chew our food like
likkle pickney?'

It was Inez.

'No suh,' she carried on, crossing her arms.

'No one's expecting you to stay quiet for more than a
couple of minutes,' said Frank, earning a fist bump from
Clarke, and glares from Betsy and Judith.

'You know, Frank, there's this saying I follow that might
help you in future,' Betsy piped up, the sternness in her
high-pitched, mouse-like voice giving Clarke and Frank pause.
Intonations of the accent she'd picked up in Jamaica were
barely there, but gave her that famous lilt every few words.

Frank checked her for signs of impending danger. Betsy was young but she was respected in a way that meant her judgements cut deeper than most. Her integrity, succinctness and beauty – smooth, coffee-brown skin in a small frame, made all the more endearing by round, brown button eyes, bow-like lips and high cheekbones – meant she was someone you wanted to keep happy. Letting down someone so good would hurt.

'Mmhmm,' Betsy continued, taking a sip of the wine she'd poured, looking into Frank's eyes, unsettling him. 'Yes, Frank. I think it may help you and your likkle friend going forward,' she added, shooting a quick glance at Clarke, who avoided eye contact. A middle-aged man, reduced to an infant.

Betsy licked her lips and smiled before continuing, the delivery of each word plain as paper:

'Respect your elders.'

Mikey, sitting to Betsy's right, laughed loudly along with Inez, who always appreciated Betsy's efforts to defend her.

'That's right!' Mikey echoed, pointing at Clarke and Frank. They'd busied themselves with shaking their heads in mock shame. Clarke changed the subject.

'Well, Mikey, as my elder. I respect you for inviting us all for dinner tonight. Now, respectfully boss ... sir ... weh the food deh?'

There was roti, rice and peas, curry chicken, plantain and callaloo, followed by sickly sweet potato pudding and coconut ice cream. Save for the ice cream, Mikey had cooked and baked it all. He'd burned and tossed pieces of plantain and pots of rice to get the end result. It was waiting in the kitchen for his guests, wafting spices and heat in their direction.

Mikey asked if they were ready to eat. They nodded in unison, lingering before offering to assist Mikey in the kitchen, Betsy's words about respecting elders still ringing in the minds of the men, who'd ignored it. As Judith talked down the two women from getting up to help – 'you cook for us every day, don't you think you deserve a rest?' – Frank and Clarke battled it out for the title of least wutless.

'No my breddah, siddung, ah my turn fi plate up,' Frank said, making a show of his helping.

'"No breddah",' parroted Clarke, deepening his voice to match Frank's.

'Relax, mi nuh mind!'

Inez and Betsy rolled their eyes and shook their heads. Neither could be bothered to help in that moment.

'I think Frank makes a good point,' Inez piped up, her usually forceful voice coy to the point of humour. 'It would be nice to be waited on, for once.' Frank smirked and nodded at both of the women, aware of what they were getting at, and got up from the table.

'My pleasure. We ain't waiting on you again any time soon, so enjoy it now,' he added, tilting his head down as a sign of respect before disappearing into the kitchen.

'Took your time,' said Mikey, who was making his way out of the kitchen with two pots of steaming rice – plain as well as rice and peas – sending the sharp fruitiness of the infused Scotch bonnet in each of them floating into the main part of the restaurant. Frank stood by to let him pass and grinned, hoping the nagging wouldn't become a theme of the evening. Judith was busy stirring the curry, which, though hot, had formed a bit of skin since it'd been sitting. The expression on her face was largely vacant but Frank saw it betray flashes of worry every now and then: a furrowed brow; widened, shifting eyes. He wondered what was wrong. But didn't ask. They carried on in silence, stirring new life into the food.

'Did he tell you about the photographs?' Frank asked, his back to Judith as he dished scalding callaloo into a dish.

'The frames on the walls?' Judith replied, still stirring.

'Yeah man.'

'No, he didn't.' Judith clapped her hands together and wiped them on her jeans. The food had long been ready to take in, but Frank's tone suggested something was off with Mikey. Off to the outside world, if not him personally. It wasn't Mikey's nature to preoccupy himself with the mundane.

Frank explained about the photos and the bizarre call to come help put them up and the secret treasure trove in the basement. Mikey shuffled back into the room. He was still talking to the guests at the table, grabbed the plantain and callaloo and made his way out again. He didn't seem to catch a word of what either were saying.

'Help me carry this in?' Judith asked, placing her hands on one side of the tray that held decanted pots of curry. Frank lent a hand, whispering a few more words about the photo situation as they gingerly backed out of the kitchen.

'When he reveal them, just ... be as enthusiastic as you can, yeah?' Frank whispered.

'Why wouldn't I? What are they?' said Judith, struggling a little with the heavy pot.

'Listen, all I can say is all dem rumours about him being some big-shot photographer might be true. Might be even better than true.'

They cut their conversation short the second they were in earshot of the rest of the guests, a silent vow to say nothing until Mikey seemed ready. He hadn't mentioned those frames all evening and was looking at them with a curious expression as they made their way back to the table.

Once they were all seated, Inez led the group in prayer. It was a lengthy blessing, all blood of Christ and light and dark; thank you Lord this and in Jesus's name that. Mikey didn't mind. Though not religious, he enjoyed the pomp and circumstance that came with Inez's unwavering faith – it felt apt tonight.

Mikey smiled at his guests as they sucked on bones and sopped the rich curry with warm pieces of roti. They were having a good time. He liked being the cause of it. Even Inez, who, ordinarily pretended she didn't like to drink, was allowing herself to become tipsy on tonic wine, magnum bottles piling around her.

Mikey decided it was time and began to clear the plates. He clasped his hands together, mustering the biggest sense of drama he could, and said in a booming voice, deeper than usual:

'Now, for the main event.'

The guests exchanged glances, widening their eyes and drooping their mouths in mock surprise, wondering what Mikey had up his sleeve. He walked over to the covered frames, beaming at them as if the sheets of paper obscuring the images beneath were pieces of art themselves.

'Frank, will you do the honours?' said Mikey, gesturing to a footstool next to the first photo as Frank saluted him and set to work removing the tape from the edges of the frame. The photos underneath looked like masterpieces, the revelation of each inspiring gasps from the group. Illuminated by lighting usually reserved for the local promotional posters, they felt both warm and arresting. There was one of a crowd of Black people on Portobello Road, a woman in a towering headscarf smiling back at the suited man behind her. Next to it, a collage of snapshots of Mangrove Nine trial protestors, defiantly holding up signs reading: 'FREE DARCUS HOWE' outside the Old Bailey. The weight of the history of it all caused Inez's jaw to drop. A flat-capped Black woman with short natural hair poking out the sides, posing on scaffolding as she gazed down the lens, was the third. Between the woman's beauty and the evident intimacy of the shots, the guests wondered aloud whether she'd been a former lover of Mikey's. Perhaps even a current one. He ignored all of them. The only colour photo was of the old Cudjoe's food truck, serving at Notting Hill Carnival in the late '70s, decades before any of them had even heard of Mikey. The puzzle of Mikey's existence was beginning to make sense, each photo a missing piece.

'Mikey, these are …' Judith stopped herself, drawn in once more by the history before her. She'd heard of the days when Notting Hill was uniquely Caribbean – but she'd never seen it.

'Yes! A real artist dat. You should be proud,' said Frank, shaking Mikey harder than he liked, and raising a toast. Even so, Mikey lapped up the praise, looking younger and more alive than they'd ever seen him. It may have been the alcohol: Inez was beginning to sway, and Frank's deep timbre had risen drastically in volume. But nothing about their admiration seemed affected.

After an hour of quizzing Mikey about the photos, details of which he gave sparingly, with a glint in his eye, the guests had retired to the counter for drinks. Sensing an opportunity to break away while Clarke distracted Mikey with a promise of showing him his prized records from his car boot outside, Frank pinched Judith's hand and led her quietly to the basement before anyone could notice.

'You sure he won't be vex?' said Judith as she followed Frank down the dark steps leading into the belly of the basement. The box of photos Frank had been going on about were exactly where he said they'd be.

'No sah. Mi really tink he wan fi celebrate these too one day. Him just nuh know how, or where fi begin,' said Frank, poring over the remaining photos, careful not to let his thumbs touch more than the sides.

His loving expression made Judith smile. She adored how much these men, though they wouldn't say it out loud, cared for and respected one another. But she knew Frank had a tendency to defy orders, and didn't want to rock the boat.

'Did he tell you that himself?' she asked, to which Frank, half listening, nodded. Judith kissed her teeth, standing back as he carried on.

Frank had discovered that Mikey's stories – escapades with world-famous celebrities recounted to uninterested customers at the end of the day – may not have been bullshit after all. Sensing that Judith still wasn't sold on the secrecy of it all, he explained it was for Mikey's own good.

'Him lost him confidence, Judith. Mi wan fi help him find it again. You saw how him skin him teeth up there.' Judith was touched by Frank's effort to help Mikey. Far more than a woman chaser, a gyalis, he was a loyal friend.

'Bwoi just show me whatever you came fi show me. Cah mi nah wan argue,' Judith continued, waving him on so as to hear the rest of the entertaining details about the pictures. She'd always wanted to prise open some part of Mikey's secrets. Few at Cudjoe's knew Mikey's real name. Though she'd long wanted to quiz him, Judith knew better. But cocky as ever, Frank had got this far.

'Ah whole 'eap a beautiful photos in there, Judith. Y'know all those old-timey ones? Glamorous women, famous-looking women ... and men ... even tink mi ah see Sugar Ray Robinson in there before Mikey come in and nearly catch me.'

I knew it, Judith's widened eyes seemed to say. She embraced him in excitement, eager to celebrate with everyone in a few moments' time. A loud bang interrupted them. The door had been slammed open. Mikey was standing in the doorway, glaring. As Judith looked up, she saw in Mikey a familiar expression. The same one from the party. Distant. Cold. Like thunder. She didn't understand what had caused it.

Mikey descended the stairs and wedged himself between the pair, glaring at Judith, and then fixating on Frank.

'What do you two think you're doing?'

'Mikey,' said Frank, confused and a little hurt.

'Too boring upstairs? You need fi have your own likkle secret time together?' Judith burst into laughter at the suggestion, her tittering cut short by a death-like stare from Mikey. He'd taken on an intensity that she'd never seen before.

'You likkle ...' Mikey was struggling to speak, spit flying from his mouth as anger rose within him. It made Frank want to laugh too. As a flash of amusement passed over his face, Mikey exploded.

'You disrespectful little shit,' he screamed, as Judith waved her hands and tried in vain to defuse the situation.

'Mikey, what on earth?' Judith asked. His eyes were full of rage, disappointment and creeping shame. They shifted from one person to another, searching for meaning.

'Mikey, mi a big 'oman, enuh. Mi nuh wan no likkle bwoi.'

Frank shook his head in disbelief, which grated at Mikey. He'd been sussed. His feelings spewed all over the basement. He doubled down, shifting the target of his ire towards Frank entirely.

'No steady job, constant police trouble, always asking to sleep on *my* floor. Useless piece of shit.' Judith pleaded with them both to stop, as Mikey waved her away.

'Get out of my restaurant, Frank. And don't you ever, ever come back. I'm serious. We're done. You're done.'

Frank lowered his eyes and looked at Judith, touched by the panic in her eyes. Mikey had gone too far, sent mad by his own delusions yet again. He'd meant every word of that firing. Frank knew it.

'All right, Mikey. Mi hear you. Mi gone, okay?' he said, walking past the two, mounting the stairs and disappearing into the light at the top of them.

Judith cut her eye at Mikey and followed after her friend, knowing he wouldn't be so bold as to fire her too. She wanted Mikey to know that what he had done was wrong. He deserved to feel bad about it. Perhaps he did. She took one last look at him below, and hoped the guilt would set in deep enough for him to change his mind.

Mikey shrugged and turned to the box of photos. He picked it up and stared into the cavity as if it contained some otherworldly portal, instead of his neglected personal collection. That was the last time he would be so trusting, he told himself, clutching the box to his chest so tight that the corners began to press into his skin.

Chapter Nineteen: The Flood

(Harlesden, 2011)

Betsy rarely called Judith. Theirs was a casual relationship at most, natural as it felt to both of them. When Judith saw the young woman's number light up on her phone at 6.30 a.m. that morning, she knew something was wrong.

'You heard?' said Betsy.

'Heard what? About Frank?'

'No, no. Well, yes, the customers even know about all that. But it's not that, something terrible has happened.'

Judith closed her eyes, disturbing images of death, murder and robbery playing out in her mind. Had they killed Mikey? Who was 'they'? Perhaps it had nothing to do with Mikey. Feeling her breath getting shallow, Judith prompted Betsy as politely as she could.

'Sorry, I didn't mean to alarm you. It's just that there's been a flood. Really bad. Whole restaurant done.'

'Weh yuh mean "done"? As in, it wash away with the water?' Judith was letting her fear turn into irritation.

'Let's just say, without Frank, I don't even know if the insurance will cover a re-opening. Judith, it's BAD. Kitchen done, basement done, main space basically done. The water look like it went as high as hip length. The only things that survived were up top.'

'Lord . . . anyone hurt?'

'No. No, I went in this morning and found it like that. Mikey didn't even know. He's trying to sort things with the landlord and the insurers now but . . .'

'Shit.' Judith suddenly felt white hot. She felt guilty for swearing, as if she did it all the time. She didn't want Betsy, a child, to think any less of her.

'Yeah man. It's that bad,' Betsy replied, unfazed.

'Anyway,' she continued, 'I'm just calling to pass on the message. Don't come in today. And don't bother Mikey, he's not taking calls or visitors. Nearly cussed me out like I caused the flood myself. I think it's getting to him bad.'

'Not surprised,' said Judith, making excuses to come off the phone. She felt angry that Mikey would refuse giving more information. It was her livelihood. She felt sad for him too. He didn't handle pressure well. The burden of rebuilding Cudjoe's, at a new location or not, would surely be too much. What about the photos? Had they survived?

'Don't visit Mikey my back foot. As if that likkle girl can tell me what to do,' Judith said out loud to herself, driven to see the damage for herself. Before she had time to think, she was putting on her shoes and coat, legging it to the bus, waiting at her stop and catching it just in time. By the time she'd caught her breath, she knew what she was going to do. Mikey never really 'took' visitors anyway. But this was an emergency. She needed him to know that she'd be there to help.

When Judith arrived at Mikey's flat, she felt as if she had made a grave mistake. He'd only cracked the door a little by the time he found his way to it, after ignoring her loud knocking for what felt like an hour. Judith looked deep into Mikey's eyes, squinting and tiny in the darkness surrounding him. He looked scared. The only other time she'd seen that expression on his face was after the fallout with Frank.

'Mi cyaan do this all day, Mikey. I'm just here to make sure you're okay. If there's anything . . .' Mikey continued staring from behind the crack in the door. He still hadn't taken it off the chain, which irritated Judith. It wasn't as if she was going to barge in. He knew that, didn't he?

A few more minutes went by, the standoff seeming more and more silly with each silent second. Then, the hurried clanking of the metal chain, as Mikey pulled the door in towards him, revealing a characteristically chaotic mess. She wondered for a second if something had happened here too, until the yellowing pages of the books everywhere gave away the rough age of the clutter. There were pieces of fabric – beautiful and rich with colour, perhaps from some part of west Africa – draped over unshapely forms all over the room; impressive, looming portraits of people she felt she should know the names of; dusty wooden sculptures of men and women, arms pinned to the sides as if they'd been petrified. He was a hoarder of this stuff, Judith thought. Of this *art*, she corrected herself, feeling the mess getting to her and trying not to let it.

'The restaurant,' Mikey whispered, staring slightly beyond Judith as she made space for herself on his sofa. 'Sorry about the mess, I haven't had a chance to . . .' he trailed off and sat on the arm rest closest to Judith.

'Nuh botha about that now. The flood. What are we going to do?'

Mikey looked defeated. 'Nothing much I can do for a little while, Judith. It's in the hands of the insurers now. I don't even know what caused it. Nobody seems to.'

'A duppy?' said Judith, trying to lighten the mood and regretting it, until Mikey grunted something that sounded like laughing. As she got up to make Mikey tea, she felt better about coming after all. He'd needed support, even if it felt unnatural to him to accept it. And she'd felt just as obliged to be the one to give it to him, because, to her surprise, this man had become her friend.

'Mikey, yuh nuh easy ennuh.'

'Mi know, mi know,' he laughed.

She slapped the side of Mikey's sofa and let out a 'hai!' knocking something loose from the tower of boxes next to her. Mikey lunged forward as if he wanted to get up to fix the mess, then thought better of it and tried to change the subject. The slight spark in his eyes was beginning to give way to worry and sadness once more. Catching this, Judith decided to pick up whatever had fallen down. She thought she had broken something and she didn't want to destroy the progress she'd made by not at least offering to clean it up. She picked up the pile, apologising for her clumsiness.

'Cha, I said I came to help and look what mi ah do. Mess up the shop.'

'It's fine, Judith, it's fine,' said Mikey, struggling to get up.

'No, you sit down. Let me.' She was on the floor now, picking up loose papers, envelopes, boxes. *The* box.

Mikey looked as if he would have tackled her to the ground the second she found it. He might have tried had it been someone else.

'Mikey is this . . .' Judith turned to look at her friend, now an ashen shade of light brown, and held up the box containing the photos he'd been so desperate to keep concealed. She knew he wouldn't fight her on it this time, because when she looked up at him, he had closed his eyes and was rubbing his temples. She turned back to the photos. They felt like tiny treasures. Touching them, even gingerly, felt much too rough. But oh, were they gorgeous.

'They're so beautiful, Mikey. I . . . I've never seen us like this. It's like we're the stars, you know what I mean?'

Mikey nodded, embarrassed, running his fingers through his coils nervously. She wasn't even looking at him now. She was transfixed. The photos had sucked her in.

'Wow,' Judith whispered to herself. 'It's like, anyone could look at these and see us for who we are deep inside. Like deep, deep. We are *art*. You made us into that. It's you alone who can make others see too.'

After an hour of talking, not talking and drinking tea, Judith made her excuses and decided to leave. She'd check in with him again the next day, to see if he needed any food or someone to talk to. There'd be no shifts for a while now, not until it was safe to go back in.

Judith left Mikey's block of flats and turned onto the high street, to a discount superstore, full to the brim with cleaning products. She went in before she could change her mind and set to picking up all the heavy-duty items she could find: disinfectant, bin liners, cream cleaner, gloves. It was the only way she could think to help.

Chapter Twenty: The Aftermath

(Wandsworth, 2011)

Weeks later, and the stains just wouldn't come out. The waves of muck embedded in every corner of the restaurant wouldn't allow it. Judith scrubbed anyway, squatting and scraping for minutes at a time on her knees, extending her fleshy arm up as far as it would go for the tricky bits higher up on the wall.

Cudjoe's was devastated. If didn't matter if she wanted to throw the towel in. It wasn't her call to make. She'd had no instructions to stay home, no sign – other than the appearance, Laad Gad, that appearance – that this was the end. So she came, armed with two full plastic buckets of heavy-duty cleaning products: disinfectant; a dust mask; her thickest rubber gloves – a green pair with impractical fluffy fringe like Kim and Aggie off *How Clean Is Your House?*, with all those dutty white people, and a prayer that everything would be all right. She wasn't ready to say goodbye to the restaurant, but she knew she had to. She hadn't been paid since the accident – and her savings would only take her so far.

She could do with the *How Clean Is Your House?* team, she thought, as she let her mind wander towards something more manageable than the demise of her job. Kim and Aggie had worked miracles in the past . . . that one with the lady and all that rat poo . . . or was it damp? Or cat sick? They all seemed to have rat poo. Nasty. Still, there was nothing a good dose of lemon juice, vinegar and a full team of cleaners couldn't fix. They'd do a hell of a lot better than the 'professional team' that'd been in already. She glared at the once pristine counter-top she'd lorded over weeks before. She peered down the blackened back stairs to the left of it, leading to the basement she used to escape to when Mikey or the customers were getting on her last nerve. The cream-tiled flooring was coming up. The lime-green paint was curling down the edges of the skirting boards. She peered closer, studying each crack and crevasse as the sight of the jagged texture sent chills down her spine. It looked like a rash, or some kind of bacteria, the way it curled up and jutted out like that. Like something in the foundations was sick – rotting from the inside out.

It'd been a long time since she felt that way – chilled with dread at the sight of something mundane, like a wall. The peeling paint reminded her of the surroundings she'd been trying to escape since she first moved to the UK. With each bump and snag that brushed against her hardened fingers, she winced. Suddenly, she was transported back to the early days of living in that tiny flat, with them, with *him*. It had been dirty, just like this place, but with a thick air of oppression, masked by the sounds of music, arguing, screaming kids and blaring TVs. The first place she called home in England was a hellish dump. As water collected in her mouth and her stomach began to turn, she knew she had to put it out of her mind.

Whatever happened to Cudjoe's next would be 'Cudjoe's' decision, Mikey's. But maybe Frank could handle the flaking mess, Judith wondered. She'd have to call him. Maybe Frank and Mikey were on speaking terms now.

Judith wondered why Mikey felt that this place was worth saving. She enjoyed putting a smile on people's faces, liked being needed – she was sure her boss felt differently. He was deep in debt, loathed the majority of the regulars and barely tolerated the ones who had put enough hours in to earn themselves an extra serving of plantain every once in a while, or the meatiest parts of the curry goat. He pored over the photos he had let decorate the place – with more affection than she ever saw in his eyes when he talked about Cudjoe's. Perhaps the flooding was a blessing. They could all finally let go, be free to do what they wanted. Where was he anyway? Why was she the only one here?

'Hai!' Mikey let out a high-pitched laugh from the doorway behind Judith, knowing it would make her shoulders and plentiful bosom jump. He'd answered her question, telepathically, it seemed.

'Why yuh always shout suh?' said Judith, kissing her teeth and moving away from Mikey. She ran her fingers along the wall and examined it for dust, as if that were the most pressing matter at this moment, rather than how any of them would pay their bills in the coming months. Anything to stop herself from melting under his comedic charm; a playful enemy and, now, a close friend. He was *playing*. Even now, when his restaurant looked to have no future.

'I'm making an entrance, Miss Judith.'

Judith rolled her eyes. 'I was looking for you.'

'Yuh always look pon me,' he interrupted. Mikey was leaning against the door frame now, like one of those 1950s

Hollywood heartthrob types – James Dean, except in the protruding body of a wiry-haired, pork-pie-hat-wearing brown-skinned man pushing seventy. He looked ridiculous, Judith thought, slapped his bent back, but not so hard that it wasn't clear she was joking.

'Yuh too fool-fool. Come on, we've got a restaurant to fix up, and I've got a class in a couple of hours.'

'Yuh never say nothing about no class, Judith.'

'I'm here on my day off, Mikey. I don't need to tell you anything. But I'll help find cover if you need.'

Mikey kissed his teeth. Judith took no notice, preferring instead to polish the same spot behind the counter. They both knew the restaurant wouldn't be opening that day. Neither of them could say the truth out loud.

Chapter Twenty-one:
The Letter

(Tottenham, 2012)

Judith got in at 9 p.m. that night after a late finish at school, as she liked to call it, followed by a later prayer meeting at St John's. They'd discussed the meaning of loyalty at length, the elders chiming in with their usual righteousness, some of the braver youngsters keeping them on their toes. What did it mean to be caring? How could we honour our bond with God through the relationships in our lives? Were we doing that at all? Pastor Lewis, a poetic man with a surly streak, his preacher's body to match, oozed authority. She was nervous around him, in the way she always was with men of God. They were admirable by nature, knew themselves and knew the Lord. It made her feel small and calm in ways that her daily life had long sapped. Lately, that serenity had stayed with her outside of the walls of the church. She could take the feeling home with her, especially on days like this, when she had it to herself. She felt safe, these days. And her course in health and social care meant she was well on the way to doing, full-time, what she'd always dreamed: nursing people back to better health.

She thought about this more while melting in the shower and dressing down for the evening. Judith rubbed Palmer's cocoa butter up and around her forearms, the oily substance leaving an almost glittery sheen on her mole-peppered brown skin. The sickly-sweet smell and soft caress of her own fingertips soothed her. She continued to trace gentle circles across her skin, like she'd always wanted someone to when she had been touched. Maybe it was a good thing that the girls were out. She hadn't let herself think about herself in this way in a while, and she wanted to embrace it with no noise or distractions, no guilt about who was on her mind. She wondered what it would be like for Mikey to touch her like that, surprising herself, shame and satisfaction permeating her sense of peace. *Was that what she really wanted?* She walked into the living room and sat upright on the edge of the plush corner sofa by the window, as if waiting to be called into the principal's office for a telling off. The cream blinds had been drawn, but she was convinced you could still see into the flat, even if it was five floors up. She checked once, twice, three times. Jumped at the sound of a rogue shriek from a child from down below, held her breath when her neighbour came crashing into his flat two doors down. 'Drunk again,' she whispered to no one.

This wasn't the right time after all. All the signs indicated otherwise. She slipped down into the sofa in exactly the way she told visitors not to: haphazardly, with no regard for the upholstery, no *respect* for this place – *chups*. The guilt began to subside. She took a quick glance around again and allowed herself to dissolve into the moment. She rarely had the living room to herself. She was going to take advantage. Kicking off her slippers, she sprawled out across the full length of the sofa and lay back. The TV was hers tonight. But where was the remote?

Not wanting to get up, Judith craned her head, searching. It wasn't under the sofa, just dust and a smushed joint that made her kiss her teeth. More searching revealed the remote poking out under a letter that someone, probably Lisa, had dropped there absent-mindedly.

'Typical,' Judith said to herself, reaching for it and flipping over the envelope by accident. She swore she'd seen her name on it. No. Had she? She bent to pick it up, bringing it to a stool by the kitchen, hoping it wasn't a missed bill. She hated being behind – in anything. The stamp and crisp machine seal on the brown letter told her it might be. It was something official, anyway. Judith flipped over the envelope and ran her thumb through a small hole by the seal, nicking her finger as she did so. She let out a hiss as the sharpness hit and brought her finger to her mouth, licking off the excess blood. Some of it smeared on the letter. She hoped that wouldn't be an issue. Pulling it from its sleeve, she recognised the letterhead immediately. A crest bearing the Queen's crown next to the words 'Home Office'.

She hadn't read a word beyond 'Judith Hyacinth Beckford', but knew it was bad already. The Home Office didn't get in touch for the fun of it. Even with her student visa, she'd heard whispers of this sort of thing in her classes. At Cudjoe's too. Horror stories about unsuspecting, law-abiding people receiving paper threats one day, and disappearing the next. She needed a break. Judith closed her eyes and tried to slow her breathing, steadying herself with one of the dining chairs. If she didn't read on, perhaps it wouldn't be real, she thought, willing delusion to take over, knowing it wouldn't. She had to read on.

Skimming past the refutation as the paper flapped against her sweaty palms, her eyes fixated on one of the last sentences on the page: 'Your application does not fall for a grant of leave to remain outside the rules.' Her chest tightened. She began to cough. The paper felt white-hot, somehow. She let it fall to the ground and watched it sail down in what felt like slow motion. Even from the floor, the words 'does not fall for a grant of leave to remain' were still visible. She couldn't breathe. Kept coughing. She skimmed the letter again. *'The Applicant arrived . . . United Kingdom on 2 January 2007, with an entry clearance as a student . . .* Your application does not fall for a grant of leave to remain.' The words made less sense the more she focused on them. She'd worked so hard already. She hadn't done anything wrong.

Delroy. Was it him? Or William, their former landlord? She wouldn't put it past either of them. But Delroy had his own visa and legal woes. And William had given the flat up so quickly that she wasn't sure it made sense for him to strike back in this way. Unless Lisa had received a letter too. Had she tried to hide this from her? Was that why it was under the sofa? Judith was beginning to feel dizzy. She stumbled and reached in vain for the dining chair again as her body continued to fall backwards. Her head thwacked into something hard – the corner of the kitchen counter. Searing pain shot through the centre of her head and she tumbled to the floor with force. She could taste the dryness of her tongue now, bile rising up her throat, warning what was coming. But her limbs wouldn't carry her anywhere – she couldn't move. *Help me*, she thought, as the pain intensified. Her vision turned to white.

Chapter Twenty-two: The Visit

(Edmonton, 2012)

The nurse said there had been visitors around the clock when Mikey finally arrived. Round the clock. He imagined a conveyor belt of gushing friends and family, dishing out hugs and flowers. He had sat motionless for a few days too long after he heard the news. Judith had been alone in her flatshare when the heart attack struck. Girls he didn't know existed before they called had told him that, as if the detail helped. It had been a week since it happened when they got in touch. Roommates of hers, they'd said. Couldn't find his number Tuesday, the day she collapsed, they'd said. But Judith talked about him all the time. They were so glad, after trying him for days, that he finally answered his phone.

Mikey had been busier than usual when he found out. He had Judith to thank for that. Her prying had pulled him out of a slump he didn't know he had fallen into, thrusting him into the arms of an adoring, image-conscious artistic crowd. Calls and emails occupied him. Requests from pushy journalists rolled in. Long-forgotten and barely known names popped up, declaring themselves his good mates, or biggest fans. It was all too much. But it was about time, too.

The heart attack, in the midst of all that, didn't feel real. It stopped the clock. No, broke it. How could anything so bad happen to someone so good?

He was lagging behind the nurse. Her sense of purpose made him uneasy. He didn't want to get to Judith's room without collecting himself. But on the professional went, thick, straight, black ponytail swinging as she strode down cold blue corridors.

'Yuh . . . yuh sure she's still taking visitors?' Mikey said, not quite loud enough for the nurse to hear and embarrassed by his empty hands – were gifts expected for this sort of thing? She stopped, turned around and smiled warmly.

'Here we are,' she said, gesturing towards the open door to her right. It was too late to back out, then. 'Judith, I've got a visitor here for you,' the nurse said cheerfully, concealing weariness betrayed only by the dark circles under her eyes. 'I'll be back a little later. Let me know if you need anything, okay?' She patted Judith gently on the leg as she turned to leave the beige, nondescript, information-poster-smothered room. Judith, hospital-gowned and frail, was lying in bed and smiling along with a twenty-something tomboy. *Must be Lisa*, he thought to himself, embarrassed that it had taken this for him to finally meet Judith's nearest and dearest. Mikey cleared his throat. Judith turned her head slowly to face him and broke out into a grin so vivacious that he wondered for a split second whether she was all better. Had she seen something or someone behind him? He turned to check.

'Yes. Ah you mi ah look pon, Mikey,' said Judith, smiling harder. Her hair had been canerowed into a simple style Mikey had never seen on her before. Someone – probably

Lisa – had greased her scalp. A detail he wouldn't have noticed had the sunrays not been gleaming off her head through the window. She looked nice. Frail, but almost younger.

'So, you must be the infamous Mikey.' Lisa, standing on Judith's left, had turned to face him with her hand outstretched and an expression that read: 'perhaps I should be leaving.' His cheeks went flush.

'One and the same,' he said, tipping his imaginary hat towards the two women and then fiddling with his silver afro, hoping to dispel any silly theories about his relationship with Judith by giving neither of them more attention than the other.

'She's been talking about you nonstop, haven't you cuz?'

Judith kissed her teeth and chuckled. 'Ignore her. Are you going to stand on the other side of the room the whole time Mikey? Mi nah contagious.'

Mikey walked dutifully towards Judith's bedside, grabbing her right hand instinctively and cradling it for a few seconds before he caught himself. He'd never held her hand before. But it felt natural all the same, their skin coming together. Too natural. Slipping his hand out of hers, he began to pace around the room in small, uncertain steps.

'Why you going around worrying everyone, huh? You need to look after yourself better. Didn't I tell you . . .' Mikey trailed off, unconvinced by his own diatribe. Judith was shaking her head with her eyes closed, laughing.

'Well, anyway. I'm sorry,' he continued, barely meeting her gaze. 'I'm sorry I didn't get here sooner. I didn't know whether . . . mi neva . . . Judith, I didn't know.'

She patted his hand and squeezed it.

'None of that matters, Mikey. I'm glad you're here. I – I've missed you.'

'I've missed you too,' Mikey muttered, hanging his head. It felt good to hear her speak to him warmly. To know she was okay. And, selfishly, okay with him.

'I'm going to take that as my cue to get a snack. Mikey, it was lovely to meet you. I'm sure we'll meet again soon enough,' Lisa chuckled, winking at her cousin before disappearing out of the room.

'So, the famous Mikey came to see likkle old me. I must be lucky.'

Mikey went slack. So she knew, then. After resisting her help for as long as he had, a decision to take the plunge and relaunch his career had led to results. He was having an exhibition. It was through the 'Black artistic elite', as he had named the handful of people who had penetrated the white art scene – and had enough influence to bring one or two people with them, from time to time.

Mikey wanted to tell Judith about his desire to have her be a guest of honour at the event. But he didn't want to take up all of her time with it. Her life had been at stake; what would she care about some swanky evening trying to fit in with people he knew she'd hate? People he probably hated too?

'Chat bout "famous". Mi nah nobody,' he added, removing imaginary dirt from one of his fingers.

'Will you come to the exhibition, though, Judith? It's in a few weeks. We can get you a wheelchair, if you need one. Something comfy to sit on?' He was rambling. It made Judith laugh.

'Mi proud of yuh, ennuh,' Judith said, surprising Mikey.

She'd become a little more forthright since the heart attack; she realised there was no time to waste.

'Yuh should invite Frank too. Haven't heard from him in a long, long time. It might be nice.'

Mikey ignored her, knowing she was right.

'Whatever you decide, mi with you. Mi know it took a lot for you to revisit this.' Judith paused and smiled to herself. 'Of course I'll come to your exhibition. I may be a likkle frail, but nothing could hold me back from celebrating you. Y'hear?'

The apples of Mikey's light-brown cheeks went flush. He knew in that moment that he loved Judith. Bending down slowly, half for his own comfort – his back wasn't what it used to be – and half because he still wasn't sure what he was doing, Mikey caressed Judith's face and kissed her gently on the lips. Eyes closed, their smiles struggled to broaden beyond their faces.

'I've been waiting a long time for you to do that,' Judith whispered, peering up at Mikey. He made her worries – all the lingering ones, about her stay, about her life – disappear in that moment.

'Could've done it yourself from long time,' Mikey replied, chuckling to himself. He had hoped this reunion would go well when he was mulling over the decision to come. But he hadn't imagined everything falling into place.

Chapter Twenty-three:
The Exhibition

(Brixton, 2012)

Mikey had spent his whole life wondering what it would be like if he'd become one of the chosen ones: a creative darling, name-dropped by acquaintances who wanted his shimmer to rub off on them. Would everything become bearable? Well-deserved recognition lifting him up and keeping him floating, higher, higher, until he felt it was time to come back down to earth? How does one prepare for a feeling like that? At his age, would he have to dredge excitement up from the pits of his youth, when hope and arrogance once came as naturally as disappointment and fatigue? He had long accepted the prospect of a happy, if slightly bitter, future of running Cudjoe's, eventually retiring, achievements far in his past. Until suddenly, they weren't.

Word had spread fast about the southwest London-based restaurateur-cum-photography genius, though why Mikey wasn't entirely sure. Though his old circles recognised him as one of many unsung heroes of the British Civil Rights era, a preserver of the sort of activism that is buried beneath general, watered-down accounts of history, those ties had long frayed. If they hadn't died, most had moved away years before, leaning into their lifelong mission to disrupt the status quo, or abandoning it for something more stable.

The whispers had started mere days after the unveiling of Mikey's collection, markers of days past that people now yearned to know more about. Caribbean west London, pushed further and further to the margins by the wealthy, felt like mythology now. Signs of its existence might be found on plaques, the odd shop front and Notting Hill Carnival; it had long come to mean only poverty and squalor. Mikey's work was about to change that.

It started with a record company. Mikey got a call at Cudjoe's from a record-label rep asking if he'd taken any early photos of famous reggae bands – bands under their management. He thought it was a prank at first. The man's plummy tone, concealed under an east London twang, had thrown him off. He had used the words 'mate' and 'innit' about ten times. He was too familiar. One of them hipsters, Mikey thought to himself, once he'd established that the call was legitimate. After setting a fee and exchanging emails, an effort that almost made him give up all together – he'd agreed to a courier coming to pick up the various photos he'd taken. By the time the courier brought the photos back, the local area was abuzz again.

'Rahtid . . . you have all these photograph here too?' Betsy said, ogling the works like treasure.

As his small fanbase began to spread, journalists came knocking, as eager to know about the man behind Cudjoe's as the photography itself. He was a local celebrity (again). Then the flood hit.

If you'd asked him then how he'd felt when he believed

the flood had washed away his livelihood, he would have said one word: 'Done.' The prospect of losing his work felt like the closest thing to a death sentence. He imagined it all slipping away from him: nowhere to display his work, no chance of strangers coming in off the street, eager to hear him spill about the famous activists he'd known, the women he'd dated, the unexpected places he'd found himself. This man was an adventurer, one of a kind. It pained him to admit how reliant he was on the praise. Yet he wanted to be there to bask in it. Cudjoe, posted on a bar stool, pretending to read a newspaper, fending off questions he'd been waiting for his whole life.

Mikey had spent the months after that spiralling. He had less money than ever. People he'd come to rely on were disappearing around him. He hadn't dared speak to Frank after their fight. Even after Judith's urging at the hospital, and in the weeks following it. Instead, he'd let his pride swallow him up, preventing him from doing anything more than yearning for a friend he now realised he'd wronged. A friend he didn't blame for not wanting anything to do with him, even after trying, multiple times, to get in touch with him.

Still, however much the rejection stung, it pushed him towards something equally valuable: a chance to connect with a generation he had written off. It's curious how life works, Mikey remembered thinking when his next bout of luck came along. He'd been posted up at Windrush Square at Brixton Splash, watching the crowd sway along to Busy Signal's 'Jamaica Love', shaking his head. In the buzz of the crowd, he'd initially mistaken the song for Alphaville's 'Forever Young', and kissed his teeth when it came on, thinking it inappropriate for a celebration like this, on Jamaica's fiftieth year of independence from the United Kingdom.

'Why is the DJ playing this tune? Is it 1984?' Mikey said to a group of twenty-somethings next to him, the few people who hadn't joined in with the singing, because they were too busy chatting. One of them, a short fat girl sporting the neatest, blackest afro he'd ever seen, with a small beginner's DSLR hanging off her neck, turned to him and smiled politely. He could tell she'd had no idea what he said, and was about to embarrass her for it, but something made him stop and smile back anyway. The camera, for one. But it was her styling too. On her white T-shirt, there was a black-and-white print of Sade's *Love Deluxe* album cover. He'd never cared for the artist, and suspected the young woman didn't know too much about her either, but he appreciated her wearing Sade's face like a badge of honour – an homage to her parents' generation, probably. They continued that way for a short while, him muttering to himself and her forcing grins for his sake, as her friends paid neither of them any mind, avoiding the risk of being pulled into respecting one's elders. When a tall, greying man grabbed Mikey's shoulder and called him Cudjoe, the girl's ears pricked up. She listened as he talked about 'the old days', gallivanting with supermodel Donyale Luna, rubbing shoulders with Hakim Jamal, Duke Vin. About the photography, the record company who'd paid him for his work, even the whispers of the exhibition he'd been in talks about – talks that had since gone quiet. Mikey, who had been watching the girl from the corner of his eye, could tell from her craned neck that, though she didn't know the names of these people, or the details of what they were talking about, she was impressed. When his acquaintance had left – Vernon, he thought his name was – it didn't take long for her and a couple of her friends to ask questions.

'You're a photographer?' she said, holding out her meaty palm for him to shake. Her hands were softer than satin. Never done a day's hard work in her life, Mikey thought, a tad ashamed of his quickness to negativity.

'I am.' Mikey was puffing out his chest now, the once disinterested friends of the girl now suddenly up for chat with an old man, now that he was valuable to them.

'I'm a photographer too,' she said as her eyes shrank behind her cheeks from smiling so much. 'My name is Sasha.'

By the time Sasha became Mikey's assistant, Mikey's photos had appeared in another book, a joint effort between him and a Guyanese writer called Ike who wanted to document 1960s Notting Hill, using Mikey's photos to illustrate his findings. The curators started rolling in, approaching him for more exhibitions. His team of one became four, a mixture of cultural experts and creatives who'd dedicated their lives to preserving and amplifying the works of artists like him. Artists who had been rendered irrelevant, no matter how brightly their talents shone.

Mikey was everywhere: at the Tate Britain; in podcasts; in long, gushing feature articles. His team complained of the volume of emails. Britain, hungry for his contributions over half a century later. But days before the opening of his biggest exhibition yet, at the Victoria and Albert museum in London, he couldn't stop thinking about what he owed to everyone who'd encouraged him to get to this point. Frank, in particular.

Wanting to tell them, to invite them all down, he tried Inez first, a harmless buffer before the main event. The muffled burr on the other end of the line seemed to ring on in perpetuity. There was no voicemail, it just rang, taunting him, making him wonder where Inez, who'd gone into retirement after Cudjoe's folded, was spending her days. It seemed he'd let everyone slip away in the years since, as frequently as he thought about them. He tried enlisting his assistant Sasha's help initially, thinking Clarke would probably have Inez's details, much as they couldn't stand each other. But he didn't have enough information to give her.

'His last name can't be "sumpmn"', Uncle Mikey. Clarke what?' said Sasha with all the patience in the world. He couldn't tell her. Anything and everything to do with that place had long been lost, or stuffed into boxes in his unceasingly cluttered flat. But then, a week after he'd left a frantic message on her voicemail, Betsy called him back.

'You haven't heard, Mikey?' Betsy said, her voice heavy and detached at the same time. She'd been glad to hear his voice at first when she played his voicemail on the dash to the tube from work in the city; nothing about Mikey had changed. It was only when he began to ask questions about Inez that her composure fell away. He didn't know. When she called him back, reaching him at home, they'd spent the first ten minutes catching up on the good days, the worst days, all of it rosy-coloured, no matter how shitty it had been when they were living it. Then Betsy came out with it:

'She has Alzheimer's, Mikey. She's living in a home now. I visit her sometimes, but ...'

'She nah remember? Her mind gone already?'

Mikey's chest began to tighten. He steadied himself and lowered himself down into his sofa, clutching at the leather armrests, scuffing the fabric. He didn't hear a word of what Betsy said next, something about Inez's children, how sad they'd all been when it first happened, and how it wouldn't be long now.

'You know, until she ...'

Mikey made a joke about Betsy always being morbid and wishing death upon people, and prepared himself to hang up.

'But Clarke, Clarke will know w'appen to Frank,' said Betsy, slipping back into the accent.

'I have his number still. We don't talk, really. Haven't for years. But you can try him, you never know!'

Chapter Twenty-four: Ghosts

(Clapham, 2013)

As the napkin sat ignored by the dresser next to his bed, Mikey's frustrations grew. For days he moved through his surroundings as if the air were made of treacle: sticky and nauseating. After an uncharacteristically rain-filled summer, even for Britain, the humid weather was beginning to get to him. It was too muggy to think. He fixated on the fate of his lost friends; his own failure to try harder to find them; police-centred coverage about the 'riots' the year before, and nothing about the man they'd shot and killed; Britain's smugness over the Olympics ... and what was all this talk about immigration and how bad it was? Everywhere he looked, it seemed the British fear of foreigners stealing jobs was back in vogue. It reminded him of his teenage years, incensed by injustice; brutalised by the forces causing it.

This country will never change, Mikey thought to himself one October evening as he flipped back and forth between news coverage. He vented about ITV's *News at Ten*. 'Feels like a gossip mag,' he'd say to Sasha in the morning. His true issue was with Trevor McDonald, who hadn't presented it in years. It didn't stop him from ranting about him and his knighthood, a trap he felt too many had been suckered into accepting.

'All these Black people bowing to the Queen and her teefing empire,' he'd say. 'They'll send you back the moment they've had enough of you. Fools.'

Back in the day, Clarke and Frank had been his favourite audience for rants. Frank would chime in with a cheeky grin and some devil's advocate remark that no one, least of all him, truly believed. Clarke, easily baited, would become incensed, cussing out Babylon and all its incarnations, while Mikey and Frank tried not to laugh. Thinking about them made his stomach turn. He still hadn't called. Still hadn't invited them to his exhibition, which was due to open in the new year. He wanted them there more than anyone, even extended family. *They're the ones who know hard work. How this country can ruin you and ask for a generous tip afterwards*, he thought.

Picking up the napkin, tattered through months of neglect, he stood up to try Clarke on the number that Betsy had given him. Barely making out the digits beneath the stains, he tapped them into his house phone, letting his thumb hover over the call button for a second, then mashing it before he had a chance to change his mind.

The phone had barely rung when Clarke answered.

'Mikey?' he asked, recognising the name that hadn't appeared on his call list in years. Mikey let the silence pass for a few seconds too long, scrambling to come up with the right thing to say. When he eventually spoke, his own calm voice surprised him.

'Long time, Clarky, long time,' he began, sounding confident while terrified. Clarke didn't pick up on it.

They laboured over all the mandatory topics with the ease of two people who spoke every day. How sad it was that Inez had gone senile, what a shame it had been that they hadn't all stayed in touch. Never any blame. He took the good mood as a sign it was okay to invite him to the exhibition. Clarke accepted eagerly, offering compliments Mikey struggled to take. Mikey felt relieved. He wasn't such a terrible person after all. He began to tune out, preoccupied by what the warm reception might mean for his chances with the others. *Maybe it won't be so bad. People lose touch, it's life,* he thought.

'Yeah man. It's a shame what happened to Frank,' Clarke continued, shocking Mikey out of his dazed state.

'Weh yuh say? W'appen to Frank?' Mikey asked.

'Him in prison. Or a detention centre. Mi nah know which one, but him lock up for sure. Ran into his daughter Charmaine at Charing Cross Station one Friday evening . . . or was it Thursday? Might have been the afternoon, you know.' Mikey breathed out through his nostrils in frustration. Clarke had always been one for useless details.

'And what happened next? She tell you him lock up?'

'She filled me in a likkle, but I could tell she didn't want to talk too tough, you know?'

As Mikey's heart sank, he bobbed his head up and down.

'Yes it . . . must have been difficult for her,' he added, as a piercing ringing in his ears began to drown Clarke out.

'Mmm. She gave me her mooma number, though. Gina, you know Frank's babymother?'

Mikey grunted yes.

'Yes, she tell me Gina know more, but mi nah call 'ar yet. Mi nuh know her well enough fi just . . . call. What if she hangs up?' Clarke took Mikey's silence on the other end as a sign of disappointment in him.

'I will, though, soon,' he added.

'Give me her number if you still have it. Maybe I should call too,' said Mikey, still distant. He felt responsible somehow. Frank had been in trouble with the police before, but it had been years. He had a sinking feeling that had all changed after the flood, when he fired him and left him to rot. After Clarke passed on Gina's details, the two men said their goodbyes, lingering on the phone a little afterwards, as if it might be the last time.

Mikey raced to call Gina. He wouldn't do it if he didn't now, when the adrenaline was pumping. When she answered, he felt immediate regret. Here he was, accosting the mother of many of the children Frank could no longer support, as if he hadn't played a part in making things worse for all of them.

He'd opened with news of the exhibition, knowing Gina hadn't the room to care, though she did try to humour him with well-wishes. She sounded like she hadn't slept in days. Her voice was low energy and gruff.

'I'm sorry, Gina. If there's anything I can do . . .'

Gina ignored him.

'I'll text you the address where he is at the moment. Colnbrook Immigration Removal Centre. Maybe you can try calling the switchboard, or sending him a letter?'

'I will,' Mikey replied, a little hurt that she hadn't talked about visiting hours. It wouldn't be a stretch if Frank didn't want to see him. 'Thank you for talking to me. And again, I'm so sorry.' Gina sniffed and murmured a quiet thanks that sounded a little hostile. 'Don't blame you,' he said to himself in the quiet of his flat after hanging up. His guilt had ballooned. He had to talk to Judith. But it was getting late and he knew she'd be sleeping. They could catch up at the exhibition, and forever after that. Their kiss weeks before had played in his mind in a hyperromanticised loop.

Chapter Twenty-five: The Show

(South Kensington, 2012)

Mikey could barely sleep the night before. His nightmares were consumed by horrific scenarios that made him sweat and cry out through the night. He'd slip on stage, or stumble over his words, exposed as a clumsy idiot who got lucky. He worried Judith wouldn't show, realising that being romantically involved with him was a mistake. There were the visions of the photos themselves sabotaging things. Would they appear too on the nose? Amateur? He didn't want his work to blend into all the other wank that was out there. He didn't want it to represent too much either. He'd had enough of being told that he was 'changing Black history', or 'making history'. He was telling stories, telling the truth. But what if he wasn't as good as his peers said? They loved him, would say anything to him. These white people didn't know any better. They'd jump on any Black person if there was buzz around them. Who would be honest with him? He'd called Judith that night to find out. At three in the morning, she wasn't best pleased to have been stirred, but she sounded happy to hear from him.

'I'll be right up front, cheering you on,' she'd said, her voice warm and weary, calming him. 'And if you say anything chupid, I'll give you the eye too.'

The reassurance had sent Mikey into the deepest slumber for three hours before he had to get up. Now, twenty minutes away from the opening in the vast expanse of the V&A, he wondered what was holding Judith up.

'All set, Mikey?' Sasha, always attentive, asked while he was in a trance, gazing at the white, bare area for his big speech. He'd been coiffed and pulled so much that he felt restricted. Suits were never his thing. Why Sasha had insisted he wear one he didn't know. He'd gone along with it. He just wanted it all to be over.

'We'll get you miked up in five, yeah?'

Mikey nodded, watching guests enter the space. They were a multi-racial crowd, with a handful more Black people than other races, laughing among themselves with the confidence that comes with belonging in the upper echelons for long enough. Many of them wore Ankara, or Kente cloth, others opted for more traditional suits and dresses, clip-clopping on the glossy stone floor like a team of horses. Mikey began to get excited. Though the stuffiness was beginning to grate, he liked the idea of talking to all these people afterwards, showing Judith off to them. It didn't matter now that she was late; he needed her for the rest of the evening more.

'Ready, Mikey? They want you up front now.'

Mikey shuffled towards the event organisers and curators, shaking their hands through brief smiles.

'We're just going to do a quick introduction, and then

the floor is all yours, Mikey,' the over-eager trio assured him.

Ignoring them, he whispered: 'Sasha, can you call Lisa and ask where Judith is?' before taking position, the bustling crowd hanging on the words of the spectacled event organiser who was now introducing him.

Mikey could barely peel himself away after his speech. They swarmed him, thanking him for his candour and no-bullshit attitude, for his praise of the local Caribbean communities that allowed him to photograph them, and the woman – what was her name? – who helped to encourage him to re-enter the art world in the first place.

'Judith,' Mikey spat at the over-familiar guest, handing him his empty champagne flute as he went to find Sasha. Judith still hadn't shown up. He still hadn't settled into himself. Maybe she was still angry, after all.

'Great work, man,' a book editor he'd been speaking to for months said as he pushed past him.

'Yeah man, will catch you later,' he lied, struggling down the vast steps of the museum and out into one of its gardens. Sasha liked a cigarette. No doubt she'd snuck out.

She was outside. Perched against a stone replica in a black off-the-shoulder figure-hugging velvet dress, she was clutching her face and blowing smoke upward with her eyes closed. Her thick hair had been slicked back into a bun, her stretched curls forming subtle waves all over her head. She looked beautiful. Devastating. Devastated. Mikey thought twice about approaching her. Whatever call she was on looked private. He didn't want her to feel suffocated by him.

He knew how demanding he could be. As he thought about turning to walk away, Sasha opened her eyes and lowered her head, spotting him across the courtyard in the distance. Mikey waved. Sasha offered a tentative flap of the hand back and began to walk towards him reluctantly.

'What happened, Sasha?' Mikey said, taking his assistant's hand into his. She was shaking now, though it may have been the crisp, cool air. She wiped a tear away and looked off into the distance and nothing. Mikey could practically see her forming half-sentences in her mind and discarding them. She'd never been this quiet around him.

'We should talk about this later, Mikey,' Sasha finally said, a wax-fake smile on her face. He knew she didn't want to go into it and wouldn't push her to. Patting her on the back, he pulled her in for a half hug and tried to reassure her, telling her everything would be all right, not knowing what he was promising. He could feel her breaking with each attempt. It wasn't working. He tried again.

'Sasha, whoever hurt you, whatever happened, I'm here. I may be an old man, but mi cyaan still rumble, okay? Now, which likkle bwoi trouble yuh?'

Sasha began to sob. She could clearly no longer look Mikey in the eye.

'Mikey. It's Judith . . .'

'Judith?' It didn't make sense. Why would Sasha be crying about this? She barely knew the woman, beyond hearing Mikey talk about her all the time.

Sasha led Mikey to a bench towards the far end of the courtyard and hugged him as they sat down, shaking her head in disbelief as more guests made their way outside in the distance. The night was going well. For everyone else, if not them.

'Mikey, Judith died this afternoon.'

In that instant, Mikey was sure his heart had stopped too.

Epilogue

(Notting Hill, 2013)

'Mikey, you're really killing it, you know?' George Lane exclaimed from his large, cold office. There were no curves in this room, only metallic colours and sleek edges, shining covers of framed photography-book art, and neatly polished awards on the stacked bookshelves. George could smell an opportunity. He had when he'd first discovered Mikey, then still a failed restaurateur and forgotten relic, now a superstar, a darling.

He hadn't met anyone like Mikey, though he was used to the temperamental nature of artists. George's day involved white artists and photographers. 'Ethnic' pieces weren't his thing. But this guy's story – full of celebrity titbits and unearthed pieces of history – was incredible. He had to be a part of the journey. He had to shape it.

'They want documentaries, man. Films. You name it. We need to think of the best way for this book to really secure that, you know?'

Mikey nodded, not listening. He was having trouble concentrating on much of anything, these days. It was an apathy that George had been trying to shake him out of for months.

Now they had finally met all their deadlines, and things were on track, he couldn't allow Mikey to withdraw.

'So many ways we can approach this thing,' George added, smacking his teeth between sentences and occasionally rubbing his thumb under his nose. He cradled the egos of these people like babies, placating them as a mother with a newborn, offering them favours and opportunities in exchange for co-operation. They always believed they knew best. He just had to convince them his commercially viable visions had been theirs all along. Mikey might take some more work.

'I mean, really, brother, who has photos of Elizabeth Taylor just sitting in their back pocket? Who else? Huh? Mikey, you absolute legend. You're sitting on a gold mine.'

Mikey's face dropped. Why this man kept trying to push him away from the plan he'd laid out several times before he didn't know. The book cover was for Judith, for Frank; they deserved to be the stars of it. He was beginning to get angry.

'Look, there's nothing to say we still can't have this book celebrate all the locals you want, right?' George continued, thinking himself an effective handler. 'We *want* to showcase er, Caribbean ... you know, Jamaican culture and all that. Real, authentic Black Britain ... patties, reggae music, all that. But we need to think big for the cover. One of the celebrities. Any Bob Marley shots in the archives?'

Mikey scratched his white beard. He'd let it grow out in the year since Judith's death – his hair too, now falling down and around his face in short, squat dreadlocks. Everyone assumed he'd gone all spiritual because of grief and depression, that he was a Rasta now. In truth, he'd stopped giving a fuck.

The suit he wore the night Judith passed would be his last. The hair combing and shaving and faff had died along with her. He needed to be himself, like she'd always encouraged him to be.

'No,' Mikey said. He liked watching people's reactions when he shot them down like this. Amid the pain that still raged within him, it amused him to still have wit and dryness in his arsenal.

'I'm sorry?' George forced out a laugh and readied himself to launch into his spiel again.

'I said no.'

'But—' George sat back in his chair and seemed to get smaller.

'This book is a love letter to all the people who made me who I am, you hear? What the fuck has Bob Marley got to do with that?'

George's mouth was agape now.

'Mikey, I get what you're saying, I do—'

Mikey began to stand up with a little difficulty. In his frayed, washed-out dashiki, a pale green now after years of washing, he looked like a spiritual leader. Exactly the kind he would have laughed at in his wilderness years. Perhaps he had misjudged them. He made his way to the door.

'—maybe, maybe there's a way around this. This doesn't have to be an open and shut discussion.'

Mikey was at the door now, one sandalled foot out of it, tapping impatiently.

'George. Mi love you. Mi do. But you don't know who you're talking to. This is the last time I'm going to say it, or I'm out – okay?'

George gulped and nodded.

'This book, my work – it cyaan run unless Judith an' Frank there front and centre. There is no book without them. There never would have been.'

Acknowledgements

My entire family (in and outside of Jamaica and Antigua)

    Doreen Gohagen

    National Organisation of Deported Migrants

    Ivan Mulcahy

    Sharmaine Lovegrove and everyone at Dialogue Books

    Akin Adekeye (thank you for always pushing me to believe in myself)

    Anne Taylor (I'll always appreciate your endless support, bonus aunt)

    Sarah Bodenham and Sam Leach (couldn't have asked for better friends and housemates when I was writing. Love you both)

    Elaine Bowes

    Kenneth Taylor

    Luna Rupchand (best English teacher ever)

    Barbara Blake-Hannah

Bringing a book from manuscript to what you are reading is a team effort.

Dialogue Books would like to thank everyone who helped to publish *Soon Come* in the UK.

Editorial
Sharmaine Lovegrove
Adriano Noble
Eleanor Gaffney

Contracts
Stephanie Evans
Sasha Duszynska Lewis
Isabel Camara

Sales
Megan Schaffer
Kyla Dean
Dominic Smith
Sinead White
Georgina Cutler-Ross
Kerri Hood
Jess Harvey
Natasha Weninger-Kong

Design
Nico Taylor
Meg Shepherd
Sara Mahon
Sasha Egonu

Production
Narges Nojoumi
Amanda Jones

Publicity
Corinna Zifko

Marketing
Mia Oakley

Operations
Rosie Stevens

Finance
Chris Vale
Jonathan Gant

Copy-Editor
Edward Wall

Proofreader
Jon Appleton